"Ida, we must go to see Inspector Corcoran right away. There is no time to lose." . . . "Now?" I said. "We are going to see him now?"

"Yes. Get your coat. I shall hurry down to the front desk and ask for a taxi."

Mrs. K walked quickly to the front door. But before she could open it, someone on the other side began pounding on it. Oy, such a *tummel*! I reached past Mrs. K to open it, but she grasped my arm and stopped me. The loud knocking continued.

"We cannot go that way," Mrs. K said, pushing me back from the door.

"But you know there is no other way out, except the back window...."

I suddenly had a vision of another time, another window, when we needed to get into an apartment at the Home to find important evidence. Getting Mrs. K through that window, from *bristen* at one end to *tuchis* at the other, was like pushing two pounds of chopped liver into a one pound jar.

"No, Rose," I said, "we are not climbing through another window."

Praise for *A Pain in the Tuchis*

"This is a great detective story, filled with Jewish references and humour. A delight to read. I highly recommend it to anyone who likes their murder mysteries to be solved by the elderly Jewish equivalent of Sherlock Holmes and Doctor Watson."

~ Splashes into Books

"This book oozes with charm, humor, and mystery all rolled into one. This is a pure joy to read."

~ Socrates Book Reviews

"A relaxing cozy mystery as comfortable as a warm knitted shawl on a cold winter night."

~ Mallory Heart Reviews

"If you are looking for a great mystery that will keep you reading way past your bed time then you need to read this book."

~ Laura Collins

"I have read a lot of cozy mysteries, but I have never read a mystery story as funny as this one."

~ BabyMo

A Pain in the Tuchis
A Mrs. Kaplan Mystery

by

Mark Reutlinger

A Pain in the Tuchis, A Mrs. Kaplan Mystery

COPYRIGHT © 2021 by Mark Reutlinger

Cover Art by *The Wild Rose Press, Inc.*

The Wild Rose Press, Inc.
PO Box 708
Adams Basin, NY 14410-0708
Visit us at www.thewildrosepress.com

Publishing History
First Edition, 2022
Trade Paperback ISBN 978-1-5092-3873-6
Digital ISBN 978-1-5092-3874-3
This book was originally published by Random House/Alibi. This is a newly revised edition.

Published in the United States of America

Dedication

For Analee and Elliot, with love.

A curse? You should have a lot of money, but you should be the only one in your family with it.
—Ernst Lubitsch

Chapter One

I should have suspected all was not quite kosher with Vera Gold's death when one of the men carrying her body accidentally tripped at the front door and almost spilled poor Vera onto the ground. This was not a good omen.

Vera died at the close of *Yom Kippur*, the Jewish Day of Atonement, when we're called upon to examine our lives, confess the bad things we've done the previous year, and ask both God and the people we've wronged to forgive us. In her life Vera had much to atone for and many of whom to ask forgiveness; but knowing Vera as I did, I had no doubt she was unrepentant to the end.

About Vera's death, you might say I had mixed feelings. I was not entirely sad to see her go, although I would have preferred that she left us upright rather than horizontal.

"Ida, it's going to be a lot quieter around here now that Vera has died," said my friend Rose Kaplan as we watched two burly men put Vera into a hearse.

"You say that as if it's a bad thing," I replied. "The kind of excitement Vera caused I can do without, thank you very much."

"I suppose you're right," Mrs. K said. "Still, you have to admit Vera kept things pretty lively at times."

Now that was an understatement. And when Mrs. K made it, she and I had no idea just how lively things were about to become.

As I've said before, death at the Julius and Rebecca Cohen Home for Jewish Seniors is not what you would call an unusual event. Sad, yes. Unusual, no. Given the average age and state of health of the residents, it is perhaps surprising we aren't having memorial services on a daily basis. Nevertheless, Vera's was definitely a strange death. But then, Mrs. K seems to attract strange deaths like a dog attracts fleas.

Only fleas are a lot less dangerous.

****

"Did not your David used to blow the shofar on *Rosh Hashanah* and *Yom Kippur*?" Mrs. K asked me one day last September, the day before *Rosh Hashanah*. That's the Jewish New Year and the beginning of the High Holidays, the ten-day period between *Rosh Hashanah* and *Yom Kippur*. David is my late husband, may he rest in peace.

We were in the kitchen of the Home, helping to prepare two of the most important foods for the coming holiday, apples and *challah*. There were just four of us, Mrs. K and I and Karen Friedlander and Fannie Kleinberg. Everyone likes to eat the goodies but only a few are willing to help make them. Karen and Fannie, and of course Mrs. K, you could always count on.

You may know that, unlike celebrating-type holidays like *Pesach*, *Purim*, or *Chanukah*, with parties and presents and noshing lots of food, on *Yom Kippur* we are supposed to eat nothing at all. Instead, we fast for the whole day, from dusk to dusk. But maybe to make up for that, on *Rosh Hashanah*, we eat very well.

The apples we were cutting up to be dipped in honey—it's so we should have a sweet year—and the challahs we were making were round ones. I'm not sure why the *challah*—that's a braided-up egg bread, it makes wonderful toast—is long in shape on *Shabbos* (that's the Sabbath) and round on *Rosh Hashanah*. Some people say it symbolizes the circle of life, others that it is a crown because God is the King of Kings. Whatever is the shape or why, it tastes very good.

So while we're slicing and mixing, somewhere in the building we hear someone practicing on the shofar, the twisted ram's horn that is blown as part of the High Holiday services. When Mrs. K asked her question, I suddenly felt sad and stopped working for a moment. "Yes, that's right," I said. "For many years David was the *baal tokea*, the shofar blower, in our synagogue. I can remember him getting so excited the week before the High Holidays, making sure his lips were in shape for all the work they would be doing, just like if he were a famous trumpet player who was preparing for a big recital."

"David I never heard, of course," Mrs. K said, "but I remember one of the men who blew the shofar at our synagogue. *Oy*, such a sound he made. You know how, at the end of the final service on *Yom Kippur*, the shofar sounds *Tekiah Gedolah*, that very long note?"

"Do I know? You should have seen the color of poor David's face when he blew that note. I was always afraid he might pass out, collapse right there on the *bimah*." (That's the raised platform in a synagogue from which the rabbi leads the service.) "In fact, I once asked him please to be less dramatic and not hold the note for so long. He said he could think of no better way to die than to be accompanied by the sound of the *shofar*. After that I *really* worried."

3

Mrs. K laughed. "Yes, I see what you mean. And most *shofar* blowers, they hold the note for a few seconds and then give up. We all get the idea, and it's quite satisfactory. But this one man in our *shul*—a handsome fellow, not particularly tall or heavy, just ordinary build—would take a deep breath, begin to blow the long note, then turn slowly around, sending the sound to all parts of the sanctuary. You expected that after maybe twenty or thirty seconds, he would run out of air, like most people would. But he just kept on and on, sweeping the shofar back and forth, until we were all on the edge of our seats, wondering how long he could go on without collapsing. It was like he was Joshua at the battle of Jericho—you know, bringing down the walls with his shofar. When he finally did run out of breath and had to stop, we all felt like clapping, but of course one does not applaud during the *Yom Kippur* service. *Nu*, we contented ourselves with congratulating him afterwards."

"I'm glad my David didn't try anything like that," I said. "It maybe wouldn't have hurt him, but it would have given me a heart attack for sure."

I began to get a *bissel* watery in the eyes, thinking about David. Mrs. K knew what was the matter—she doesn't miss much—and she came over and put her arm around me. "I know, Ida," she said. "I miss my Sam too. But we must be grateful for the wonderful memories we have, and for our children, who will carry on the family after us."

"Yes, I'm being silly," I said. "It's just that at this time of the year... But we should get back to work, or there will be no apples and no *challah* to *nosh* on after services."

How important is family, I thought, especially at these times when we come together to celebrate or observe a special occasion. They provide you comfort, understanding, and hope for the future.

But not always. Standing there in the kitchen that day, I of course didn't know that in ten days, when the High Holidays had ended, Vera Gold would have passed, and how differently her family would figure into that sad event.

****

The Julius and Rebecca Cohen Home for Jewish Seniors is probably like most such establishments, except most of the residents—not all, but most—are Jewish. They serve kosher food, and we celebrate all the Jewish holidays. If you want Christmas and Easter, no one will object, but you probably are in the wrong place. Mrs. K and I have lived at the Home for several years now. The residents are a real mishmash of people: old, not so old; rich, poor; athletic, arthritic. Mentally, many of the residents are still, as they say, sharp like a tack; but some are now more like the other end of the tack, having been hit with the hammer of life much too often. You know, missing a few candles from their *menorah*. Alas, it is life in a retirement home.

I suppose Mrs. K and I fall somewhere in the middle in all of these ways, with one big exception: If we are measuring how well our minds are working, Mrs. K is definitely the sharpest tack in the box. There certainly is no doubt she's smarter than I am; otherwise, it would be me who is solving the murders and she who is telling you about it.

So I shall do the telling, as usual.

****

Vera Gold moved into the Home maybe five years ago, more or less. From the beginning, she was a real pain in the *tuchis*—you know, what my son Morty would call a "pain in the butt," and my grandchildren would use another, shorter word—always finding ways to irritate or infuriate the other residents.

I will give you some examples of what I mean.

First, there was the time Vera told Mr. Pupik, the Home's general manager, that Rena Shapiro was keeping a cat in her room. Now, this technically is against the Home's rules. Perhaps Vera knew about the cat because her room was right next door to that of Rena, and she had heard the cat meow at some time. In fact, most of the residents knew Rena had a cat, but no one minded because it was poor Rena's only companion, and besides, it harmed no one, including her neighbor Vera. Rena is a sweet little woman, frail like a *faigeleh*, a little bird. She usually keeps to herself, seldom venturing out of her room except for meals or a walk in the garden. Who would begrudge her the company of a little cat?

Apparently Vera would. For some reason—perhaps just to be mean—Vera found it necessary to let the cat out of the bag, so to speak, reporting Rena's secret to Pupik.

Mrs. K told me Rena had shown her a letter she had received from Pupik, all formal looking, saying something like, "If you do not get rid of the cat, we will have to get rid of you." Or words to that effect.

So how, you may ask, did we learn that it was Vera who snitched on Rena? Well, it's difficult to keep such a thing secret in a place like the Home, especially when there are ladies like our Mrs. Bissela living there. Mrs. Bissela, the Home's resident *yenta*—you would say busybody—doesn't miss much that goes on, and she delights in telling whoever will listen what she has heard or seen. She certainly had no hesitation telling us what Vera had done, although I don't know how she found out. It's as if she has a spy in every room of the Home. Maybe she does.

Now, in strict Jewish law, it's a terrible sin to spread gossip, which is called *lashon hara*, an "evil tongue." In fact gossiping is right up there with the big sins like murder or adultery, because of the serious harm it can do to another person. And this is even if—and maybe especially if—the words spoken about someone are true. False words can at least be proven to be false, and so the harm is mostly undone. But once a harmful truth is told, there is no way to untell it, and of course it cannot be proven to be false. As an old Chasidic tale says, once words are released into the air, they are like the feathers from a pillow tossed into the wind, drifting in every direction and impossible ever to recover.

It is also a sin to listen to gossip, because if no one were to listen, the gossip could do no harm.

So you see that Vera's telling on Rena was not just unkind, but it was a major sin. And so was Mrs. Bissela telling on Vera. Perhaps both of them will someday be rubbing elbows on the other side with *ganovim*—crooks—like Albert Capone or Bernie and Clyde, who I understand were very bad people indeed.

Why, you may ask, didn't we just refuse to listen to Mrs. Bissela's gossip? When Mrs. Bissela passes along something she has heard, it is extremely difficult simply to ignore what she is saying, sin or no sin. Perhaps we are not strong enough to resist listening. And besides, it is not so easy not to listen. Should we cover our ears and shout "ya-ya-ya" like when we were children and didn't want to hear what our parents were telling us?

Come to think of it, that might work.

Anyway, Mrs. Bissela is particularly fond of Rena, and once she found out that it was Vera who gave her secret away, she was so angry we thought she would *plotz*, burst. And she made sure everyone else knew also. I am surprised she didn't borrow a bull's horn, or whatever you call that thing which makes your voice very loud, and announce it at dinner. I was present when she wished on Vera a *mise-meshune*, a particularly violent death.

When we learned about Vera's complaining to Pupik, everyone was quite angry with her, especially Rena, as you would expect.

"There is no way Rena, who has no remaining family, could move out," I said to Mrs. K. "Where would she go? And without her cat, she would be so lonely and unhappy." I myself am not so fond of cats, but I know that some people get very attached to them, as did Rena to hers. *Nu*, to each his own.

Although we all would have liked to help, no one was quite sure what we could do for Rena. No one, that is, except Mrs. K. She is not one to stand by and wring her hands crying *oyoy vey iz mir*—woe is me—when she faces a problem. It's more likely her hands will be busy helping to solve the problem.

"Ida, we simply cannot let Pupik evict Rena," Mrs. K said to me the day after we learned about Rena's dilemma. "I have an idea. I shall look into it and see what I can do."

When Mrs. K says she will see what she can do, I consider it as good as done.

That was all I heard about Rena until the next day. We were sitting in the lounge enjoying our morning tea—nothing fancy, just Mr. Lipton—and after we had both had a few sips and settled back on the sofa, Mrs. K says, "Ida, I did a little research, and I may have found a way to keep Pupik from evicting either Rena or her little cat."

"How? You will make the cat invisible?"

"Yes, that would work, but it won't be necessary. Have you ever heard of such a thing as a 'service animal'?"

"You mean like a dog that a blind person uses to get around? What has that to do with Rena's cat?"

"I think it can be argued that the cat is also a service animal," says Mrs. K.

That sounded a bit *meshugge* to me. A bit crazy. "A service animal? That cat? What service? The lazy thing does nothing all day but sleep on Rena's windowsill. Not only does it not lead her around, she has to carry it across streets."

"Nevertheless," Mrs. K replied, "I think there's a good chance. I was reading that these days many different animals can qualify as service animals. Dogs, cats, hamsters, turtles—I don't think it matters, if they are necessary for the owner's health. And if it is a service animal—a service cat, in this case—it's against the law for Pupik to refuse to let Rena keep it."

I was still skeptical, but I know better than to contradict—or underestimate—Mrs. K.

"Okay, so the cat is a service animal. But how do we convince Pupik of this?"

"It says in the statute I looked at that it requires a doctor saying the cat is essential for Rena's 'physical, mental, or emotional well-being.' I shall speak with Dr. Menschyk about it today and see what can be done."

Arnold Menschyk is the doctor who takes care of many of the residents at the Home. He is also on call for emergencies, and you can be sure that any place in which a hundred people live, most over the age of seventy, has more than enough emergencies to keep a doctor busy.

Before lunch, Mrs. K telephoned to Menschyk's office and learned that he would be visiting the Home in the early afternoon. She arranged to speak with him for a few minutes before he began his rounds. The two of them talked for at least fifteen minutes, and when I asked Mrs. K afterwards how it went, she looked pleased but said only, "We shall see."

What we saw was that apparently it was successful, Mrs. K's talk with Menschyk. Soon after, we saw Menschyk go into Pupik's office, and not long after that they come out, Pupik looking more than usual like he has just sucked on a lemon. Menschyk passes by where we are sitting and gives Mrs. K a little wink with the eye, which is unusual for Menschyk, who generally has the same impassive expression whether he is telling you your bursitis is cured or you have three days to live. Did I mention that Rena was a nurse before she retired? Perhaps that gave Menschyk a slightly warmer feeling toward her than otherwise.

Whatever the reason, it turns out that after his talk with Mrs. K, Menschyk told Pupik that, in his opinion, Rena having a cat is necessary for her mental and emotional health, and that therefore he would classify the cat as a "service animal." After that we never heard a peep from Pupik about the cat or Rena being evicted. All we saw was the steam rising from Pupik's ears whenever the subject was mentioned.

So the cat stayed, but that was not the end of the matter. Not only did Mrs. K's intervention make a little worse an already poor relationship between her and Pupik, but Rena confronted Vera in the dining room the next day and there was quite a hoo-hah, Rena threatening to "get even" and calling Vera names we would not have thought she even knew, much less ever used. She even threw in a Yiddish curse that I had not heard in many years but am particularly fond of: *Vaksn zolstu vi a tsibele mitn kop in dr'erd un di fis farkert!* It means: "May you grow like an onion, with your head in the ground and your feet in the air!"

And after that Rena never again spoke to Vera.

****

Here is another example: Vera Gold also was a chain smoker. Now the Home is what you call a smoke-free premises. It is even against the law to smoke there. Vera was a heavy smoker when she arrived, and only reluctantly did she agree to the rule that smoking was not permitted, even in her room. This is because it's almost impossible to keep the smoke, or at least the smell of smoking, confined to the place where it's coming from. It's always making its way out to where others have to enjoy it too. Therefore the only place at the Home where smoking is permitted is in a certain area outside, to the left of the front doors. There the management has set up a nice wooden bench and a large container with sand in it. People who absolutely must have cigarettes are able to go outside to this area, sit on the bench, and smoke as many cigarettes as they wish, only putting the used ones into the sand and not on the ground for others to step on. It's true that when they come back inside they smell like walking cigarettes, and their clothes might have on them *schmutz* from where they are dropping their ashes, but most residents are too polite to ask them to take a shower and change their clothes.

This smoking area is a pleasant enough place for them to use during warm weather, but not so much in the winter. So one day about a month after the incident with the cat, about which I was just telling you, Mr. Pupik is walking by Vera's door and his nose begins to twitch, like my son Morty's always did when I tried to serve him gefilte fish. I know it was twitching, because as it happens, Mrs. K and I were passing in the other direction just then. Pupik stops us and says, "Do you ladies smell anything peculiar?" We twitch our own noses, and then Mrs. K says, "To me it smells like cigarettes smoking." I add, "To me, also." Because that is exactly what it smelled like.

Pupik nods, says, "Yes, it does," and proceeds to knock very loudly on Vera's door. Mrs. K whispers in my ear, "This should be interesting." I had to agree. So we just waited. We weren't in any hurry anyway, and a little drama livens up the afternoon.

It took a long time before Vera answered the door. She was not holding a cigarette, but as soon as the door was open the smell got much stronger, so it was obvious what she had been doing.

Pupik asked if he could come in, and although I could not hear exactly what Vera said or what excuse she made, evidently the answer was "no."

But Pupik does not give up so easily, especially where a possible violation of his rules is concerned. He said to Vera, loud enough so we could hear quite clearly, "Mrs. Gold, it is obvious you've been smoking in your room again. I've had several complaints about it lately. It is disturbing the other residents, particularly those whose rooms are nearby. As I have repeatedly told you, smoking is a health hazard for those who have a sensitivity to the smoke, and in any case it is against the rules of the Home. It will have to stop."

Mrs. K raised her eyebrows to me and we waited to hear what Vera would say, expecting her to apologize or at least promise not to smoke in her room again. But we were very much mistaken. Even though there was a smell coming from her room like the inside of a saloon—in which I have never been, but I'm sure it can be pretty *farshtunken*—Vera actually denied she had been smoking, and she even accused the other residents of making up stories against her. In fact, she used a Yiddish word to describe her neighbor Rena that I will not repeat here in polite company.

"So if you were not smoking, what is that smell of smoke that is coming from your room?" Pupik demanded.

"I have burned a pot on the stove, that's all," Vera replied.

You have to admire the *chutzpah*, do you not?

By now Pupik was getting very red in the face—in fact, even the back of his neck was red, as Mrs. K and I could see. But he somehow kept his voice under control, for which I have to give him credit, and said to Vera, "Mrs. Gold, if there are any more complaints about your smoking in your room, you will be asked to leave the Home. As I have said, it is a health hazard and a violation of the rules. Good day."

And with that he turned, gave us a very unfriendly look—as if we were part of the problem—and continued on his way.

"I would not like to be Pupik's next appointment," I said.

I don't know whether Vera was afraid of being evicted, or maybe she just wanted to avoid any more visits from Pupik—who wouldn't?—but as far as I know there were no more complaints, and after that Vera did her smoking only on the wooden bench by the front doors.

She didn't look happy out there.

****

Just to show you that Vera was what you might call an equal opportunity pain in the *tuchis*, she didn't confine her abuse to residents or management. Ordinary employees came in for as much mistreatment as anyone, perhaps more. Vera could make a waitress cry, the gardener swear—it seemed to come naturally to her.

I remember the morning I heard a commotion on the lawn at the back of the Home, just behind my bedroom. I peeked out my back window and there was Vera Gold, standing in front of the machine that mows the lawn—it was one of those funny-looking contraptions, like from a marriage between a big tractor and the little push mower my father used to have, with a seat in the middle and handlebars like a bicycle—waving her arms and yelling at the man who was sitting in the seat. I couldn't tell what she was saying, but it was obvious she was not wishing the man good morning. The driver, a very large man whom I didn't recognize, looked like he was trying to get in a word for himself but was having no success. Finally, Vera stalked away, still looking angry, and the man went back to his mowing, but not before he made with his hand a rude gesture. One she couldn't see, of course.

When I passed Vera in the hallway about an hour later, I asked her what the kerfuffle on the back lawn was about.

"That idiot had the nerve to run his infernal machine right under my window this morning and wake me out of a sound sleep," she said. "So I got dressed and went right out there and told him in no uncertain terms where he could put his lawn mower."

I suppose Vera would have been justified in being so angry, if it were not for the fact that this mowing about which she complained took place at maybe ten o'clock in the morning. Not everyone can conform to Vera's sleeping schedule, but clearly she didn't see it that way.

Another time an employee named George Williams, a quiet, good-natured gentleman whose job it was, among other things, to make the rounds of the residents' rooms each day to empty the wastebaskets, accidentally left one of the wastebaskets in Vera's room just inside her bathroom door instead of in the corner where it belonged. Vera was not there at the time. When she returned and apparently was in a hurry to do her business, she tripped over the wastebasket.

Fortunately, Vera was not hurt, and apparently she even got to the toilet in time. But you would have thought poor Mr. Williams had deliberately tried to injure her, and that she had fallen and broken several bones, to hear the way she berated him as soon as she found him. "You idiot," she said in front of several of the residents, "I could have been killed. How much *saichel*"—common sense—"does it take to put the damn wastebasket back where it belongs?" And other kind words.

Now everyone would agree that this man made a mistake leaving the wastebasket where it didn't belong, and he probably deserved a warning from his supervisor to be more careful. But it was obviously unintentional and something anyone might do during a busy day, and that should have been the end of it.

Not for Vera, however. After finishing with George, she marched into Pupik's office and demanded, loudly enough that several nearby residents heard her, that the poor man be punished in some way. In the end, he lost a week's salary, a significant amount for anyone, but especially for a man raising four children. And maybe the worst part was that it was still his job to empty those wastebaskets every day, and whenever Vera was in her room at the time she would take the opportunity to remind him of his mistake, and not in a kindly way.

Everyone felt sorry for George, except Vera, of course, who probably considered his punishment a victory for herself. But there was nothing we could do to change Pupik's mind. So as usual, it was left to Mrs. K to come up with at least a partial solution. She collected a little money from several of the residents, including the both of us, and gave it to George. It was not the full amount he lost, but I'm sure it helped and he appreciated the gesture.

"When I tried to give him the money," Mrs. K told me, "at first he refused to take it. But I convinced him that we all wanted him to have it, and that we thought Vera's overreaction to what he had done was unforgivable."

"I imagine he's still quite upset at Vera," I said.

Mrs. K laughed. "Upset is not the word. I could see he was trying to keep his words under control, but I would say it's a good thing he's not a violent person. At least I hope not. When I mentioned Vera's name, he became very angry and burst out that 'God will punish her.'"

It sounded as if George wouldn't have minded doing the job for Him.

****

So you can see what kind of person was this Vera Gold. Not easy to live with, and making enemies faster than Mrs. K makes matzoh balls, which is very fast indeed. Vera also had mood swings that were hard for others to predict. Sometimes she could seem happy and friendly, other times almost depressed. Nevertheless, most of us made the effort to get along with her, as we all live close together and it's better to put up with occasional troublemakers than to let them poison the atmosphere for everyone. And when she was not making trouble, Vera could actually be quite an interesting person. She was well-educated, spoke several languages, and had traveled to many unusual places when she was younger. Her stories about these travels were fascinating, even though Mrs. K and I both suspected she was maybe embellishing them a little.

"The storyteller must keep his audience interested," Mrs. K once said after listening to one of Vera's reminiscences. "If he strays a bit from the truth to do so, well, he is not, after all, under oath." And I had to agree. It may be that truth is sometimes stranger than fiction, but it's usually more interesting to hear from a person's imagination than strictly from his memory.

Chapter Two

It was in June, I think, a few months before *Rosh Hashanah*, that Vera Gold became quite ill. I don't know exactly what was her ailment, but she took to her bed and Dr. Menschyk called in a specialist of some kind to examine her. Whatever it was he prescribed, it seemed to do Vera much good and, although she still spent a lot of time in bed, or at least in her room, most days she was able to join the other residents at meals and in the lounge or the garden. "I'm much too tough an old bird to stay down for long," Vera said to Mrs. K and me one sunny day in the garden. "I'll go down kicking and screaming, I can tell you." I think we all believed her. It certainly looked like whatever had tried to knock her down had failed miserably.

Almost from the time Vera arrived at the Home, her son, Daniel, a pharmacist, would come to visit her regularly. In fact, he would be there almost every afternoon after leaving the pharmacy and before going home. "If it weren't for my Danny living in the community and working so close to the Home, I never would have come here," Vera said shortly after she moved in. Of course she then had to add, "There sure isn't much else to recommend this place." *Nu*, that was Vera. Would it kill her to say something nice? Perhaps.

As he was at the Home nearly every day, we all got to know Daniel quite well, including Mrs. K and myself.

He seemed to be a real mensch, a good person, very friendly. And he was very attentive to his mother, even before she fell ill. Vera, in turn, never said a bad word about Daniel, at least not that I ever heard. She obviously loved her son very much.

Mrs. K and I both enjoyed talking with Daniel when we had the chance and found he had both *saichel* and a nice sense of humor. But Mrs. K always took a special interest in him. I believe it was because he reminded her of her own son, named Adam, who had planned to be a lawyer. He joined the Air Force, which after he served would have paid for his law school tuition; but he never got the chance: He was on a reconnaissance mission somewhere overseas when his plane went down, with no survivors. (*Zikronah livrakhah*—may his memory be for a blessing.) Mrs. K seldom speaks of her Adam, whom I didn't know, and I don't ask. But I have seen pictures, and Daniel Gold has a close enough resemblance to make me feel certain she sees a lot of her son in him.

Even before her illness to which I'm referring, in fact as long as we knew her, Vera had a whole alphabet soup of pills that she took in the morning and evening. She was one of those people who, when they travel, have to carry an extra suitcase to hold all the medicines. Generally the Home's nursing staff would help residents with their medications, but Daniel had decided from the time his mother moved into the Home that he would help her with her evening pills.

"I'm here every afternoon anyway," he told Mrs. K, "so I might as well be useful. And I'm sure my mother would rather I give her her meds than a stranger do it." This was no doubt true. Vera clearly appreciated his looking after her that way, rather than some busy staff person. Daniel became very familiar with what Vera was taking so he could be sure she got the right medicines, in the right order, at the right times. And of course being a pharmacist himself, he would know better than anyone about such things. But despite this, they actually made him and Vera sign a paper saying that the Home would not be responsible if Daniel gave his mother the wrong medicines. "Isn't it ironic, Ida?" Mrs. K said. "As a local pharmacist, he has probably filled most of those prescriptions himself, maybe even these very ones for his mother. I'm surprised they don't make us all sign a paper before dinner saying we will not blame them if we swallow our dentures and choke to death."

"Not so loud," I said, "or you will give them ideas."

And so Daniel became what you would call a regular fixture at the Home, sometimes even staying for dinner with his mother. It was good to have a younger man around as almost a part-time resident.

About a month before *Rosh Hashanah*, Vera's illness—or maybe another illness not related to what she already had, I don't know—became much more serious. Mrs. K and I went to see her in her room, but she was too ill to talk to us. It was probably the only time since we had known her that we could be sure she would not speak ill of anyone.

This time whatever Dr. Menschyk had given her before did not seem to help, and he again had to call in a specialist, with whom he conferred several times. The specialist prescribed some new medicine, which she was to take every evening with, or just after, dinner, together with the medicines she was already taking. Daniel of course insisted on being the one to give Vera her new medicine together with her other pills and potions when he came to see her in the late afternoons. Given the seriousness of Vera's illness, the Home was more reluctant than before to let Daniel do this, but both he and Vera insisted. "I think I'm capable of helping my mother take a few pills," Daniel would say, and of course he was.

They made them sign another paper.

****

Now living also at the Home for perhaps two years before the time we are speaking of was Vera's younger sister, Frances Kleinberg, of whom I have already spoken as helping out in the kitchen. Fannie, as everyone called her, was in her mid-sixties, almost twenty years younger than Vera. In fact, she was probably the youngest resident of the Home when she arrived, having just lost her husband and wishing to be closer to her remaining family, as she told us. Other than Fannie, Daniel, and Vera, apparently there was only a cousin who, I thought I had been told, was living in Singapore. But no one had heard from him in many years.

Fannie lived in one of what are called the "independent" units at the Home, a separate building with nice big apartments that are meant for people who can take care of themselves but don't mind someone else preparing their meals, cleaning their apartments, and so forth. They also might prefer living with other people, particularly Jewish people, rather than by themselves. There are maybe twenty such apartments at the Home.

Fannie was quite different from her sister, Vera, like maybe honey cake from gefilte fish. I was telling you earlier that here at the Home there are all types of people among the residents, and a good example of this is the contrast between Vera and her sister. Where Vera could

21

be abrasive and mean-spirited, Fannie Kleinberg was, like her nephew Daniel, a nice person: friendly and helpful. Like most of the residents, when you think about it.

There was quite a difference between the sisters physically, also. Vera was tall and thin, always looking like a strong wind might blow her over. She had a sharp nose and a narrow forehead. She generally wore her hair fairly long and was always well-groomed. The overall impression was, however, as Mrs. K put it, that "all she needs is a pointy black hat to play a witch on Halloween." I guess her looks fit her personality.

Fannie was tall, but she was, you might say, not particularly thin. She had a round face and rosy cheeks, with short blond hair. She didn't seem to worry much about her appearance, often wearing clothes that didn't quite fit, that seemed too loose. I have noticed so many ladies of my age wearing clothes that are just a *bissel* too small or too big, because with age they have somewhat expanded or shrunk, and either could not afford or could not be bothered to buy a new wardrobe.

Given these many differences, no one would guess Vera and Fannie were sisters just to look at or speak with them. Or to live with them. But sisters they were. I only learned later that Vera was adopted, which helps to explain her being so different from Fannie.

A few days after Vera became so sick and took to her bed, we got to talking with Fannie in the Home's library.

She turned to Mrs. K and said, "You know, Rose, I'd really like to help take care of my sister, to help her with her medications. Do you think they'll let me?"

"Well, as you know, Daniel has been helping Vera

with her medicine every evening. I don't think either Vera or Daniel would want to change that."

Fannie appeared to think this over before saying, "Yes, I'm sure you're right. And I certainly don't want to interfere. But I know my sister takes a lot of medicines both morning and evening, and it must be harder for her now that she's so sick. We were always close, and I hate to see her in such discomfort and not able to do anything to help. Maybe I could help her in the mornings, just as Daniel does later in the day. See to whatever she needs doing. Do you think they'll let me?"

"I don't see why not, do you, Ida?" Mrs. K said.

"Well," I said, "Daniel is a pharmacist, so they might trust him more with the medicines."

Fannie scoffed at this. "Hey, I've taken hundreds of pills in my life, and I've given them to other people. How hard can it be?"

"Yes," Mrs. K said, "I agree. I'm sure they'll let you help if you tell them what you told us. They will see that it's best for everyone."

"But they'll make you sign a paper," I added.

****

The next day, Fannie told us she had gone to see the head nurse and had indeed been given permission to help her sister in the mornings.

"*Mazel tov*," Mrs. K said. "You see, everything was resolved for the best after all, with no one getting upset."

So a routine was begun, with Fannie taking care of Vera in the morning, Daniel helping her in the late afternoon and early evening, and the nursing staff coming in and checking on her or giving her other assistance during the rest of the day. It seemed to work smoothly, and believe me, if it had not, we all would have heard about it from Vera, illness or no illness! And it was soon apparent Vera began feeling better, occasionally leaving her bed for meals and exercise.

"It's fortunate," Mrs. K remarked to me at that time, "that it's Daniel and Fannie taking care of Vera, and not the other way around."

"No, I wouldn't want to be left in Vera's care," I said. "I wonder if she has always been difficult like this, or only in her later years."

"You know, Ida," Mrs. K said, "there could be many things in her life that made her bitter and unhappy. Maybe when she lost her husband. Maybe there were other family troubles. It doesn't seem to have affected her relationship with Daniel; at least he's clearly affectionate toward her, and he's about the only person, outside of Fannie, she's always nice to."

"Perhaps we can ask Daniel about it sometime," I said.

"Perhaps. It's not an easy question to ask."

"No, but we certainly can't ask Vera."

****

As it happened, there was more than one reason we would not be able to ask Vera.

The best care can only do so much, and on the night of *Yom Kippur*, just hours after the end of the Day of Atonement, Vera passed away.

It's true Vera had been very ill. But no matter how serious Vera's illness had been, as the old Jewish saying goes, "better ten times ill than one time dead."

Zikronah livrakhah—may her memory be for a blessing.

Chapter Three

Although it was not what I would call a great shock that Vera passed, seeing that she had been so ill, it was nevertheless something of a surprise that she died when she did. As far as anyone could tell—at least those of us who are not doctors—Vera's health had been improving, and we certainly had heard nothing to the contrary from either Daniel or Fannie.

In fact, only two days before she passed, Mrs. K and I had visited Vera in her room. It was early afternoon, when neither Daniel nor Fannie was on duty, so to speak. Mrs. K and I had always gotten along with Vera pretty well, or at least better than most of the residents. Maybe this was because we had been lucky enough not to cross her in some way. Or maybe because just about everybody gets along with Mrs. K. Anyway, we were pleased to see that Vera was in good spirits, sitting up in bed and reading. We asked her how she was feeling.

"Much better, much better. No thanks to Menschyk or that quack he brought in," Vera said. "It's a good thing I have a strong constitution or I'd have been dead long ago with the kind of care I get around here. Other than from my own family, of course." I was glad she added that last part, and that she was grateful for Daniel's and Fannie's help.

I was also glad, believe it or not, that she was her old mean self again. It meant she definitely was feeling better.

Another unsettling thing about Vera's death was that she died on, or rather just at the end of, the Day of Atonement. It's a solemn time for us, as I've said, with much contemplation and soul-searching, and a death in the Home, even of someone as unpopular as Vera Gold, added to the solemn mood. But we carried on as usual, and within a few days most of us were back to whatever normal might be. At least for a while.

The memorial service for Vera was conducted by Rabbi Rosen, the young man from the nearby Conservative congregation, as is usual by us. We cannot afford to have our own rabbi at the Home, so we borrow one when we have the need, and Rabbi Rosen is always most accommodating when he is asked. He had been given personal information about Vera by Daniel and Fannie, and he made a nice little speech about all of Vera's good points. He managed to make her sound like quite a wonderful person, or at least someone you would want to know well; and to be fair, I'm sure the Vera that we knew at the end of her life was not who she was for all of the years before. As I've mentioned, she traveled extensively and had many interesting adventures. She met her late husband, Gershon, in Israel at about the time of its independence—they both had volunteered to help with Israel's defense when five of its Arab neighbors attacked the new country virtually on the day it was born.

Vera was married to her Gershon for over fifty years. Perhaps it was only after her husband died and her health began to fail that she became the unpleasant person we knew.

The rabbi also said that Gershon was a successful businessman who provided well for their family. Vera must have inherited a large amount of money from Gershon, and she clearly was well off when she died. The rabbi didn't say that, of course, but we all drew that conclusion for ourselves. Unlike fellow resident Daisy Goldfarb, however, who uses any excuse to show off her expensive clothes and jewelry, Vera dressed plainly if stylishly and never so as to indicate she had more money than anyone else. It didn't seem important to her, and of course it was not to us. (Well, maybe it would have been to Daisy.) But now that she had passed, any money she had would be in her estate, a fact that became extremely important in the days that followed.

Vera's death was attributed to what they call a heart irregularity, brought on at least in part, it was assumed, by the disease she was fighting. That certainly seemed logical, and in any event, there was no other likely explanation, other than plain "old age," to be offered. We all went about our business, and I have to admit that I, and no doubt many other residents, were secretly a *bissel* relieved, not that she was deceased, of course, but that she was no longer causing us *tsuris*, no longer a troublemaker. When Mrs. K, who had not been particularly bothered by Vera on a personal level, remarked that she had been a "troubled soul who we can hope is now in a better place," one resident, who shall remain nameless, responded unkindly, "As long as it is not in this place."

****

After Vera's burial, Daniel was sitting *shiva*—mourning—for seven days, as is traditional following the death of a parent or other close relative. There is a lot of ritual that goes with this, but I'll just mention that Daniel stayed at home and observed most of the requirements.

Although by tradition Daniel was not to work or leave the house during the week of mourning, he did have to go in to the pharmacy a few of the days when they couldn't replace him.

During this period of mourning, it's common, and expected, that friends and relatives come to visit, to offer condolences and comfort the bereaved. It's a *mitzvah*, a good deed, to do so. Mrs. K and I visited on several occasions, and we saw there many others from the Home, including Fannie, of course, who spent a lot of time there with Daniel during the week, both of them graciously receiving visitors.

It is also traditional for visitors during *shiva* to bring food to the mourners, so Mrs. K brought some of her wonderful matzoh ball soup and I baked a very nice *challah*, the long kind, like for *Shabbos*. Food is not the answer to grief, of course, but as they say about chicken soup, it can't hurt.

****

A death at the Home always causes a disruption of our routine—sometimes more, sometimes less—that lasts for a few days at most, and then things return to normal. In Vera's case, by the next day most of us were ready to move on without her.

Mrs. K and I were just finishing our breakfast—she a bialy with a *shmear* of cream cheese, I a hard-boiled egg and toast with a *bissel* jam—when Fannie Kleinberg comes over to our table and asks to sit down. There was plenty of room, since Mr. Isaac Taubman and Karen Friedlander, our usual table companions, had already finished and excused themselves, so naturally we invited Fannie to join us.

Of course, we had already expressed to Fannie our

sympathy at Vera's passing, but we again told her we were sorry for her loss.

"Yes, thank you," she said. She looked quite sad.

"It must be very hard losing a sister, especially one you were close to," said Mrs. K.

"Yes. But it's in a way comforting to know that we did all we could for her, and she had the best of care."

Mrs. K reached out and patted Fannie's hand to show she understood. Fannie turned to Mrs. K and said, "I especially appreciate your support, Rose. A lot of the people here were less than friendly toward Vera. Oh, I know she could be a difficult person to get along with, but that was mostly her illness; she was really a good person. But you were always nice to her and treated her like a *mensch*. You too, Ida."

"It's true your sister could be…as you say, difficult," Mrs. K said, being diplomatic, "but we all have our own *mishegoss*, our own bit of craziness, and it's best not to judge others too harshly, especially when they're dealing with serious health issues as Vera was." She didn't mention, of course, that Vera had been a pain in the *tuchis* from the time she arrived.

"Yes, Rose, and it's those health issues I want to talk to you about."

Mrs. K looked quite surprised, as was I, and said, "Her health issues? Isn't it Dr. Menschyk with whom you should be talking about them? All I know is a person gets a sickness, and sometimes the sickness leads to their passing. Beyond that, it's all a mystery to me."

"That's just it," Fannie said. "I don't believe Vera's illness, as serious as it was, led to her passing, as you put it."

Again Mrs. K and I were surprised.

"Pardon me," Mrs. K said, "but are you saying your sister died of what they would call 'natural causes' despite her illness? Not that it matters at this point, I suppose…"

"No, no, that's not what I mean," Fannie said. She lowered her voice and leaned closer to us. "Maybe I should just come right out with it. I think it's possible Vera did not die of natural causes at all, or of any disease.

"I think someone killed her."

Chapter Four

It was quiet at the table for maybe a minute, as Mrs. K and I both tried to digest what Fannie had said. I think it was giving both of us indigestion. There were a few residents of the Home who one might expect to make such an odd statement, or for that matter any statement, such is the condition of their mind; but Fannie Kleinberg was definitely not one of them. If anything, she was among the least likely to do so.

Mrs. K was the first to speak up. "Now, Fannie, are you seriously suggesting that someone here in the Home murdered your sister?"

Fannie looked entirely serious about it. "I know it sounds crazy," she said, "but let me try to explain."

Mrs. K put out her hand to indicate Fannie should not explain just yet. "Wait a minute, dear. I don't know what you have in mind, but it sounds like something you should be telling to the police, not to me and Ida."

"Yes, I understand, but it's really not that simple. First, I don't have the kind of evidence the police would be looking for, as strongly as I believe I'm right. But also I remember how you outsmarted the police and got to the bottom of what happened to poor Bertha Finkelstein. It was about the time when I moved into the Home, and everyone was talking about it."

Mrs. K waved off this reference to Bertha's mysterious death at that year's Passover *seder*, a time none of us will ever forget. In truth, this was not the first time since then that someone had come to her for advice in some kind of "mystery," if you can call "where could my keys have gone?" and "who took my fountain pen?" mysteries. Nevertheless, she had definitely developed a reputation for being able to solve crimes, as if she is Mr. Sherlock Holmes himself, whom she admires very much.

"I'm sorry, Fannie," Mrs. K said, "but I really am not the person to whom you should tell this story. It is a real policeman you want."

But Fannie was adamant. "Please, Rose, just listen, and then I'll do what you think best. At least it will give me a chance to put the facts before someone who I know can look at them logically, which is difficult for someone like me who is so close to the matter emotionally. Will you listen?"

Mrs. K smiled and took Fannie's hand. "Since you put it that way, Fannie, if it will make you feel better to tell us about it, we are certainly willing to listen, are we not, Ida?"

Fannie had not directed her appeal to me, of course, but now she looked at me to confirm that she could continue her story.

Who was I to say no? Besides, Mrs. K might be able to resist hearing what Fannie had to say, but I was much too curious to do that. So continue she did.

****

"As you know, my sister Vera had various medical problems over the years, although until recently none of them has been what you'd call serious, at least not serious enough to put her in the hospital or to threaten her life. In addition to some physical issues, she had some mental problems, which probably accounts for at least some of the behavioral peculiarities you and others would have noticed."

Actually, I didn't know about this mental problem, and I don't think Mrs. K did either, not that we would expect to. One doesn't usually announce to the world her medical problems, especially if they are of the type to cause others to look a bit sideways at you.

Mrs. K nodded, and Fannie continued: "I had been taking care of Vera during her latest illness, helping her with her morning medicines and generally seeing to her needs in the early part of the day."

This we knew. "And it was very kind of you to help her that way," Mrs. K said. "It's not always true that a sister or brother—or any family member, for that matter—is willing to take on such a responsibility."

"Oh, it wasn't so much," Fannie replied. "Not compared to, say, a child who has sole responsibility for an aged parent's care. That can be the most difficult job imaginable. But yes, it isn't always the case that relatives help out. But Vera and I have always been close." She paused for a moment, staring into the distance as if picturing something in her mind.

"I remember one time when I was having trouble in school—I must've been about ten years old, and the other kids had been making fun of me, you know how cruel kids can be to each other—and Vera, who was working in another city at the time, came home for the weekend and spent almost the whole time with me, helping me feel better about myself and suggesting ways to respond to the other kids. She was much older, of course, and always the strong one in the family." Fannie smiled. "I guess that was pretty obvious even now."

Mrs. K and I looked at each other and we both

nodded. Yes, I thought, that sounds like the Vera we knew. Probably when she was in school, she was the one doing the bullying, so she would be an expert on the subject.

"Vera was very lucky," I said, "to have not only you to help her, but also Daniel."

"Yes," Fannie said. "And together I think we took pretty good care of Vera. But to get back to what I was telling you—"

Just then, one of the dining staff, Frank, came over to take away the used dishes from our table, and Fannie abruptly stopped talking. Apparently she didn't want anyone else to overhear what she had to say. As it turned out, I couldn't blame her.

Frank asked whether any of us would like something more to eat or drink. Mrs. K and I immediately said no, but it looked like Fannie was tempted. Finally she too declined and Frank went on his way.

When we were again undisturbed, Fannie continued: "Well, on the day before *Yom Kippur*, after Vera had taken her morning pills, she leaned close to me and said, 'Fannela'—she usually called me that, at least in private—'I need to tell you something. You might not believe me, but I am certain someone here is trying to poison me.'

"As you can imagine, I was totally taken by surprise by her words, and I didn't know quite how to respond. Vera had many physical ailments and also a mild case of schizophrenia, but she had never had or shown any signs of paranoia. On the one hand, such an accusation was extremely hard to take seriously, at least at the time. On the other hand, I thought, what if it's true?"

"So did you ask her for some details?" Mrs. K asked.

"Oh, yes, of course. She said something vague about some of her medications looking strange, maybe being tampered with."

"And she gave you some examples? You saw these tampered-with medicines?" Mrs. K asked.

Fannie looked distressed. "No, not really. I did ask, but Vera said she didn't have any to show me, having thrown away the items she suspected. She promised she would remember to show me first, the next time it happened. Of course, she died the next day, so she never got a chance to do that."

"Did you ask why she was telling you this? Did she want you to report it to someone, or what?"

"I think she was just afraid. She took my hand and pleaded with me to help her, to protect her. I didn't know what to say, except that I would do what I could. But really, what could I do?"

"Of course. And did you ask her if she suspected any particular person?"

"That's maybe the strangest part," Fannie said. "She first said she did, but then, as if she had changed her mind, she refused to tell me who she suspected. But just the question—that is, who she suspected—seemed to upset her more than anything else. It was as if she didn't want anyone to find out. Or maybe she just wanted to be more certain before accusing anyone." She sighed and looked down. "And maybe I just imagined she was upset. I don't know."

"Hmm. I see," said Mrs. K. I couldn't tell for sure whether that meant she sees what a problem this is, or she sees that Vera is completely *meshugge* and it's time to close the subject. But then she said, "Have you any idea what motive someone would have for poisoning your sister? I mean, she was not exactly popular, but…"

"No, she wasn't, but that's no reason someone would kill her, is it?"

"I wouldn't think so, no. Did she have a will?"

Fannie thought for a moment, then said, "I don't know, but I assume everything would go to Daniel with or without one, so that can't be important."

"No, I suppose not. So then tell me, Fannie, what do you think? Do you take what your sister said seriously?"

Fannie seemed to consider this for a moment before she answered. "To be honest, Rose, I'm not sure I did at the time, but I think I do now. When I put Vera's very real fear that she was being poisoned together with the fact that, from everything I could see and the doctor said, she was actually getting much better, and that the day after she tells me this she dies, I think I can't just let it pass without some kind of…some kind of investigation, or whatever you would call it. Some minimal attempt at least to find out if it's possible Vera was really poisoned. I mean, it's been so stressful for me, not knowing whether to try to forget what Vera said or to do something—anything—to look into it, as I'm sure my sister would have wanted."

"Yes, I see," Mrs. K said again. She now seemed to be thinking it over, her eyes focused on the table in front of her. I could almost hear the wheels turning in her head. I wish the wheels in mine turned half as fast; perhaps they have too much rust on them. Finally, she said, "I can see you are quite distressed by this, Fannie, and I know I would be too under the circumstances. I'll try to help if you wish, at least to the extent of putting your mind at rest, if at all possible."

I thought it was very generous of Mrs. K to offer like

that, because surely she didn't consider it at all likely Vera had been poisoned. Clearly she was just trying to make Fannie feel better, to help her to accept her sister's passing without feeling guilty about it. Fannie obviously appreciated it also, because she took Mrs. K's hand and squeezed it and thanked her for agreeing to help.

"Perhaps the first thing for us to do," Mrs. K said, looking a little embarrassed at Fannie's show of gratitude, "is to talk with Dr. Menschyk. After all, it's he who attended Vera during her illness, together with the specialist, and he who signed the death certificate."

"I suppose that makes sense," Fannie said. "I don't know whether he'll be able to say for sure whether Vera could have been poisoned, but we should at least ask him. Can we go to see him together?"

"Yes, certainly," Mrs. K said. "I'll call him and ask for a few minutes of his time when he's next here on his calls."

Fannie again thanked both of us, and looking somewhat relieved, she got up from the table and left the dining room, left us to look at each other in silence.

"*Nu*, what do you make of Fannie's story?" I asked.

"I don't know what to make of it, at least at this moment," she replied. "But I do know one thing: *Yom Kippur* is the Day of Atonement. It is the holiest day of the year, when we are supposed to repent of our sins of the year that has passed, ask for God's forgiveness, and promise to try harder next year.

"It would be a very bad day to commit a murder."

Chapter Five

It took a few more minutes before either I or Mrs. K could put our thoughts together. I mean, how do you react when a sensible, respected woman, not just some gullible *shmendrik*, tells you something it's difficult to believe and asks you to believe it too? Do you let her swim by herself or jump into the water with her?

With both feet we jumped in, and now we had to paddle.

So Mrs. K telephoned to Dr. Menschyk and made another appointment to talk with him, like the time I told you about, when Rena's cat was in danger of eviction. Fortunately, Menschyk is a gracious man who tries to accommodate others when he can, and such an appointment was made, for three the next afternoon in Mrs. K's apartment. We told Fannie; she seemed pleased and relieved. It was understandable.

The next morning Mrs. K and I could not discuss Fannie's situation during breakfast, because both Isaac Taubman and Karen Friedlander were there. Certainly it would be the worst kind of *lashon hara* to pass along the information Fannie had given us. But as soon as we had finished our breakfast (just a little oatmeal and some tea for me), we excused ourselves and made our way to the lounge. We plopped ourselves down on one of the soft sofas out of range of other ears and returned to the topic of Fannie and Vera.

"So, Ida, having had overnight to think about what Fannie told us, do you have any further thoughts on it?" Mrs. K asked.

"To tell you the truth," I said, "I couldn't help but wonder, if Vera was right about someone wanting to poison her, and if someone did—I know these are very large ifs, but like I said, I couldn't help myself—then who might possibly have done it, and why?"

"Hmm, yes," Mrs. K said. "And did you come up with any suspects?"

I sighed. "No, I couldn't think who it could have been. Or to put it another way, I decided it could have been almost anyone."

"Yes, I'm not surprised. The problem with wondering who did it at this point is that we don't have enough facts even to speculate. Who would gain from her death? Who might have wanted to kill her? For what reasons? And is this just a sick woman's imagination?"

"So do you then have thoughts of a different kind?"

"Not really. I was thinking last night more about the question that comes before who did it—the one you skipped over, namely, what are the chances that Vera was in fact poisoned, given all the circumstances?"

"And what did you conclude?"

"The same as you, for the same reason: not enough facts. Who had access to her food or medicine? What made her suspect she was being poisoned? Taste? How she felt? Were there symptoms that would even remotely indicate she might have been poisoned?"

"At least this last thing we'll learn this afternoon," I said, "when we talk with Menschyk."

"I hope so, Ida. If he can't give us a definite answer, we're back to having no facts, and likely to stay that way."

****

With Fannie's problem put aside for now, I picked up a copy of Hadassah Magazine and began to read a story about some big medical discovery in Israel when Mrs. K taps me on the shoulder.

"I just remembered," she said, "that I haven't yet given Lily Lipman the package of *lokshen* I picked up for her at the grocery."

"You bought noodles for Lily? Can't she buy them herself?"

"Of course, but the kind she likes they only have at one market, and I happened to be going shopping there last Tuesday, so I offered to buy them for her. I really should go and get them and take them to her."

I nodded. "Maybe I'll go with you," I said. "I haven't spoken to Lily lately, or seen her around much except at mealtimes. I might as well go and say hello."

I put down the magazine and followed Mrs. K to her room, where she found the *lokshen* after a few minutes of searching (it was hiding under a box of matzoh meal), and we then headed for the Lipmans' apartment.

Sol and Lily Lipman have one of the larger apartments at the Home, a two-bedroom intended for couples like them. It isn't terribly spacious, but it certainly is bigger than the single bedroom apartments like I and Mrs. K have, and it has a small but fairly complete kitchen.

Mrs. K knocked on the door. As we waited, we could hear what sounded like shouting inside, and a door slamming. We could also smell just a *shmek*, a whiff, of some pungent odor. Mrs. K knocked again, this time louder. More shouting, another door slamming, then everything went quiet and we heard footsteps approaching the door. Finally it was opened by Sol.

As soon as the door opened, we were struck by an almost overwhelming smell. It was as if someone had dumped a truckload of boiled cabbage in their apartment.

Sol did not look happy. You remember what I said about how opposite in appearance and temperament are—or I should now say were—Vera Gold and her sister, Fannie? Well, the same is true of Sol and his wife, Lily. And more than once, nice, easy-going Sol can be found looking like he has lost his best friend, because high-strung, excitable Lily has gone off like *shmaltz* in a hot pan. (That's chicken fat. You cook with it.) And more than once it's the bathroom where she locks herself. If their broom closet had a lock on the door, she would probably spend time in there also.

"Hello, Sol," Mrs. K said, as we both tried to ignore the odor. "I have something for Lily. Is she home?"

Sol rolled his eyes. "Is she home?" he said. "You cannot tell? You think maybe it is I who is making boiled cabbage in the kitchen? And who is yelling like a fishwife when I complain?"

"Well, no…"

Sol laughed softly. "Actually, Rose, to be fair, it is Lily's mother who is doing the cooking, and Lily who is doing the yelling."

"Lily's mother? I didn't know she was visiting you. It must be a little crowded."

Sol made a deep sigh before speaking again.

"Yes, Lily's mother lives quite nearby, and Lily visits her often, but last month she 'dropped in' for a short visit. Dropped in? More like squeezed in, like a *tuchis* in a teacup. Not only is it crowded, she has been staying with us for almost a month now. You probably have not seen her because she almost never leaves the apartment."

"Lily's mother. She would be…would be quite elderly, I assume?"

"Over ninety, I think. Yes, this is one reason she does not leave the apartment. And that is the reason I have to leave it."

"I don't understand," Mrs. K said, and neither did I.

Sol looked back into the apartment, then turned and said, "Listen, Rose, give me that package and I'll leave it in the kitchen for Lily. Now would not be a good time to bother her. Then if you both have a few minutes, maybe we could go down to the lounge and, well, you could give me some advice, like you did when Lily got so upset over that…that book I bought."

Sol was referring to a book called something like Enjoying Your Golden Years, which Lily found opened to a chapter called "Sex After 65," together with a bottle of those pills that the commercials say make men "perform better." Anyway, Lily thought Sol was "sex mad" and was *shtupping* some t*satskele*—you know, fooling around with some cute young woman—when really Sol just wanted to "reinvigorate," as he put it, his relationship with Lily. It was quite a *mishmash*.

"Certainly, Sol," Mrs. K said, "if you think we can help."

So the three of us moved to the lounge, Sol leaving his apartment quietly so Lily should not hear. *Oy*, what a way to live.

Once we were seated, Sol next to Mrs. K and me across from them, Mrs. K asked, "So Sol, what's the problem? Is Lily still locking herself in the bathroom?"

Sol smiled and said, "No, not this time, Rose. This time she says she has left me."

Now, I realize it's not that unusual for a wife to leave a husband these days, or perhaps the other way around, but not usually after almost fifty years of marriage. But it happens.

"Left you?" says Mrs. K. "Didn't you say she and her mother were just now in your apartment? And that her mother never leaves the apartment? Where did they go?"

Sol's smile now was what you would call ironic. He said, "Go? No, you don't understand. Lily is leaving me, but apparently I am the one who has to go. She says she will stay in the apartment. She and her mother."

At least this is a new script for an old production. One way or the other, though, poor Sol seems always to be the victim.

"Let me get this straight," Mrs. K said. "You say Lily is leaving you, but it is you who are leaving, because of Lily's mother, who does not leave. Is that right?"

Now by this time, sitting and listening to this conversation between Sol and Mrs. K, I'm getting totally confused. But I'm patient, because I'm confident Mrs. K will somehow clear up the confusion so that even I will understand. If not, I shall go and have a cup of tea and wait for Mrs. K to come and explain it to me.

"Yes, that's more or less the story," Sol said. "Lily wants to leave me because she says I insulted her mother."

"And did you insult her mother?"

Again the ironic smile. "Well, that depends what you consider an insult. I did call her a *kvetcher*, as she is complaining all the time; and maybe I did let slip an occasional a *khalerye*…"

"You wished the plague on her?"

"Not really; but, Rose, you don't know what that woman has put me through."

"What could a ninety-year-old woman do to you to make you, who I have never heard even raise your voice, say such things to her?"

Sol's features changed so he was no longer smiling, even ironically. He obviously was thinking of all the sins of Lily's mother.

"What could she do, you ask. I'll tell you what she could do. She takes up the only bathroom in the apartment for hours at a time—I don't know what she does in there, but I always find there enormous pieces of underwear hanging on the towel racks and shower rod—so that I actually have to go down the hall to the public restroom just to *pish*! Oh, I'm sorry, I didn't mean to say that. I mean to go to the bathroom."

"Don't worry, we've heard worse. Go on."

"Well, she criticizes or complains about almost everything we do. Like she complains we do not keep kosher, which is true, but Lily and I have never kept kosher, and it was never an issue with us."

"Well, I can understand that when someone visits who keeps kosher it's difficult when the host does not, because—"

"No, no, you don't understand. She complains we do not keep kosher, but she does not herself. She claims she would, but she cannot get kosher food where she lives. She says she should at least get kosher food when she visits us."

That woman has *chutzpah*, I'm thinking.

"And does Lily also get upset at this constant

kibitzing?"

"No, she gets upset with me for telling her mother to stop! And there's more. Did you notice what our apartment smells like?" How could we not? "She cooks things that stink up our whole apartment, like borscht made from the beets. Or boiled cabbage. Or gefilte fish. I mean, I like to eat these things, but they should not be cooked in a small apartment like ours. Certainly not several times a week."

"No, I can see your point," Mrs. K said. I nodded in agreement. No one wants to have a *farshtunken* apartment, no matter how good the food tastes.

"The last straw was when she called me lazy, because I do not work. Rose, I am retired for ten years and have no need or desire to go back to work. But this crazy woman—this *meshuggeneh*—is making my life hell."

"So was it your asking her to stop doing these things that made Lily tell you to leave?"

"Well, not exactly. Her mother was supposed to be staying with us for a few days, and now she's been here almost a month. And all this time she's been doing the things I've described to you. This morning, after she spent ten minutes criticizing what I was wearing—as if she was some kind of men's fashion *maven*—I was fed up with it and I told her she will have to leave."

"And that is when Lily told you to leave instead?"

"No, what she actually said was if her mother leaves, she goes with her. I guess I lost my temper and said 'Fine. You can both go.' Of course, I didn't really mean it, but then Lily starts crying and wailing '*Oy vey iz mir*, where will we go? What will become of us?' and, well, before I know it I am the one who is supposed to leave and Lily and her mother are to stay in the apartment with the borscht and boiled cabbage."

At least he escapes the smell.

For a little while, we all were quiet. It's a Yiddish saying that a guest is like rain: good for a little while, but inconvenient if staying too long. It appeared that Sol was by now soaking wet.

Sol was looking down at the carpet, Mrs. K appeared to be thinking, and I was simply waiting to see if Mrs. K had any ideas for Sol.

She did. "Well, Sol, if you want a suggestion, I think you should stay away from the apartment for a day or two," Mrs. K said. "I'm sure you can stay in one of the guest rooms here at the Home. As you know better than I, when Lily is in this highly upset state, there's no point in trying to reason with her. I think she will cool off in a day or two, especially if you aren't there to argue with."

"And what then? I cannot live in the guest room forever."

"Of course not. Perhaps by then I will have thought of some way to resolve your problem."

Sol looked like he was thinking it over, but after all, what choice did he really have? He was not the fighting type. I had never seen him lose his temper, even when his wife Lily went off the deep end. If he insisted on staying in the apartment now, not only would he be facing a very upset wife, but also her mother.

Two against one.

Chapter Six

At three in the afternoon, after lunch and a little nap, I knocked on the door of Mrs. K's apartment. When I entered, I saw that Dr. Menschyk and Fannie were both already there.

"Please, everyone, sit down," Mrs. K said. Her apartment is, like mine, divided into a living room (or parlor, if you prefer), a bedroom, and a bathroom. In a corner of the living room is a kitchenette, just a small sink, a fridge, and a microwave oven. There is an electric kettle for making water for tea. The living room is nicely decorated, with a small wooden dining table with four padded wooden chairs on one side and a beige sofa with matching chair on the other, separated by a small glass coffee table. Mrs. K had pulled one of the dining chairs over for the fourth person. Menschyk first sat on the sofa, but when he saw that one of us ladies would have to sit on the wooden chair, he immediately stood up and insisted he be the one to take that chair. Such a polite man is Menschyk, a gentleman from the old school, as they say. I then sat on the sofa with Mrs. K, and Fannie sat on the matching chair.

Mrs. K asked if anyone would like some tea or coffee. Fannie and I declined, but Menschyk said he had been running around so much with his calls that he had missed lunch and would not mind some tea. Fannie then said, "Well, if you're making tea, Rose, I guess I could use some," and so in the end Mrs. K made tea for everyone and brought over some chocolate biscuits as well.

When Menschyk had munched a cookie or three and washed it down with his tea, he said to Mrs. K, "Well, Mrs. Kaplan, what did you want to discuss with me?"

"Actually," she replied, "it's not just I who wants a discussion, but also Fannie, Mrs. Kleinberg, here. Perhaps it's she who should explain."

She then turned to Fannie and said, "Fannie, dear, please tell Dr. Menschyk what you told me and Ida."

Fannie looked around, seeming a *bissel* nervous, but finally she looked at Menschyk and, after glancing over at Mrs. K, told again her story of Vera's fear of poisoning.

When Fannie had finished the telling, Menschyk asked her, "So are you asking me to say whether or not your sister was poisoned? Mrs. Kleinberg, I can hardly…"

"No, of course not," Mrs. K said. "All we are asking you, as the one who treated Vera's sickness and who made the death certificate, is this: Given all that you observed, is it possible that Vera was poisoned? Or can you say with certainty she was not?"

Menschyk did not answer right away. I assume he was trying to remember all of the things he saw and heard surrounding Vera's death. We all just sat quietly and waited.

After maybe a minute, Menschyk looked up and said, "I'm afraid I can't give you a definitive answer. I wish I could. First of all, you'll understand that I cannot reveal anything about Mrs. Gold's treatment to anyone whom she didn't specifically say could be given this information."

I have heard of this problem, the "Hippo" law or whatever it is called—I'm sure it wasn't named after such an animal, but it's something like that—and in fact once when I had a bad fall and was taken to the emergency room, the doctor refused to tell my niece Sara anything about my condition, even though she is my closest relative living in this area, until I signed a paper with lots of big words saying it was okay. Another job for the lawyers.

"Fortunately, Mrs. Gold did sign an authorization for disclosure to Mrs. Kleinberg, and I don't think the fact that you two are here"—indicating me and Mrs. K—"with her consent creates any difficulty."

"So you can tell us?" Mrs. K asked.

"Well, yes, but there isn't much to tell. You asked me whether it's possible your sister was poisoned, or can I say with certainty she was not. That depends what you mean by 'possible' and 'certainty.' In my opinion, as I stated on the death certificate, your sister died of natural causes. Does that mean it was impossible she was poisoned? No, although I would consider it highly unlikely. There are poisons that mimic the symptoms of a natural death. So I cannot say that your sister's death—or that of anyone who died under similar circumstances—couldn't possibly have involved poison. I can only say I see no reason, from what you've told me, to change my original opinion. When a seriously ill woman in her eighties dies with no apparent reason to suspect otherwise, we tend to assume she died of either her illness, old age, or more likely a combination of both."

"But she seemed to be getting better," Fannie said.

"Doesn't that alone make her death suspicious?"

Menschyk smiled. "Not really. Sometimes a very sick person's condition improves just before they pass away. It's not terribly unusual. In any case, only an autopsy could answer your question with certainty."

"You mean with an autopsy you could say whether she was poisoned?"

"Oh, yes. In fact, Mrs. Kleinberg, an autopsy with toxicology would be the only way at this late stage."

"And how does one go about getting this autopsy?" Fannie asked.

"Well, if you're serious about pursuing this, it would require the consent of Mrs. Gold's son. His name is Daniel, I believe?"

"Yes, it is," said Mrs. K. "So you are saying without Daniel's consent, even if Fannie—Mrs. Kleinberg—wishes to have such an autopsy, and even with Mrs. Gold having said what she said, there could not be an autopsy?"

"Yes, that's correct. He is her closest relative and, at least under the laws of this state, the only one in a position to give the necessary consent. Unless, of course, there is a police investigation, and a court orders the autopsy."

"Well, then," said Fannie, "that shouldn't be too much of a problem. I shall explain the situation to Daniel and ask him to give his consent. Will you be the one to perform the autopsy?"

"No, that's not one of the things I generally do. It would be a pathologist. Of course, if it were the police who requested the autopsy, it would be the district medical examiner or one of his associates, and you wouldn't need the next of kin's permission. But I don't think what you have told me qualifies for that kind of…"

"Wait," Mrs. K said, interrupting Menschyk's speech, which was becoming a bit long. "It just occurred to me that, because Daniel is extremely *frum*, he may not be so willing to give his consent." *Frum* just means very religious. "He belongs to an Orthodox congregation that interprets Jewish law very strictly."

"That's true," Menschyk said. "I've run into that problem in the past, and it will depend just how religious he is, whether he shares Mrs. Kleinberg's concern, and so forth."

"I don't quite understand," Fannie said. "What would be the problem?"

"The problem would be, Fannie dear, that in general autopsies are not permitted by Orthodox Jews."

"I didn't know that," Fannie said. "Why the hell not?" She was sounding a little distressed, or maybe she was just upset by the entire discussion, because she doesn't usually use such language, at least in front of us. She stood up and began to pace up and down.

"Our family's never been that religious," she said. "We've always been Reform. This sort of nonsense is one reason why."

I should perhaps explain here that a Reform Jew is more or less at the opposite end of the religious spectrum from Orthodox. While we all read from the same Torah—you know, the five books of Moses in the Old Testament—and say the same prayers, in interpretation we are quite different. Orthodox Jews tend to follow the Torah's *mitzvot*, or commandments, much more strictly, and believe me, there are a lot of them to follow. In fact, tradition says there were 613 *mitzvot* in the Torah as handed down by Moses, including 248 things that you should do and 365 you should not do. Many, of course, are things, like to give to charity and not to commit fraud, that we all try to follow. Others, like keeping kosher in how we eat, are less widely followed by Reform Jews. But some *mitzvot*, or at least how they are interpreted— including the prohibition against autopsies—only the very religious follow. Suffice it to say, the more orthodox a Jewish person is, the more likely his actions will be subject to some kind of religious rules. *Nu*, it is the same in most religions, is it not?

But I'm going on even worse than Dr. Menschyk. To continue, Mrs. K answered Fannie's question:

"The reason is, I believe, because of the biblical prohibition against disgracing or disfiguring a body and the requirement of a speedy burial. I'm sure you know that's why Vera was buried so soon after her death."

"It also has to do with a prohibition against failure to bury the entire body," Menschyk added. "At least that's what I've been told. I remember one time an autopsy was performed on an Orthodox person and certain organs were removed for examination, but they had to be preserved and re-buried with the body after the examination. There are some exceptions, of course, such as to save another person's life, but I don't think any such thing applies here."

It was plain that this discussion was becoming too much for poor Fannie, with all the talk of carving up her sister's body and all. She sat down again and put her face in her hands. She wasn't crying, but she clearly was upset and on the verge.

As usual, Mrs. K stepped in to help. She went over and put her hand on Fannie's shoulder and said, "I'll tell you what, Fannie. You go ahead and ask Daniel if he will give his consent. Maybe we're worrying for nothing. But if he does not, then I'll go and talk with him. I probably understand the religious issue a bit better than you, so it will be easier for me to discuss it with him."

It was interesting to me that Mrs. K now seemed to have taken on Fannie's position that there should be an autopsy, although personally I still didn't think there was much reason for it. I didn't know whether she actually believed Vera might have been poisoned, of which there certainly was very little evidence, or she was just taking Fannie's part and pursuing the question as a favor to a friend who seemed in no position to do the pursuing herself. Mrs. K is like that.

Fannie looked up. "Oh, thank you, Rose. I know Daniel is very fond of you and I'm sure he'll listen to what you say."

"I'm very fond of him also," Mrs. K said. "Let's see what he tells you and go from there."

We thanked Dr. Menschyk for his time and advice—I didn't know whether we would be receiving a bill for same—and he and Fannie left the apartment.

"So, Ida, what do you think now?" Mrs. K asked.

"I think that you have stepped into a real puddle of quicksand. And I have a feeling it won't be so easy to step out again."

I didn't add that I could feel my feet sinking in as well.

Chapter Seven

After we left Fannie and Dr. Menschyk, Mrs. K told me she had promised to help Mrs. Bissela with a sewing problem she was having, so I headed back to my room by myself. On the way, an unexpected distraction came my way.

I met in the hallway Moses Klein, who everybody calls "Motorcycle Moishe." ("Moishe" is just Moses in Yiddish.) This is because he used to be one of those *nogoodniks* who wear the black leather jackets and ride around on noisy machines like a pack of hyenas, just making trouble. A *vilder mensch*, he would have been called, a wild person. Now, this is, of course, many years ago I'm speaking of, and Moishe eventually quieted down and became a successful businessman. Selling motorcycles, of course, what else? And he did it very well, they say.

Moishe still has this very large motorcycle that he parks in the Home's garage, although he stopped riding it alone some years ago. Now he only gets on it when his son, Moishe, Jr., who they call "Little Moishe," comes to visit and takes him for a ride. (I should point out that his son's given name actually is Michael: It is customary not to name Jewish children after a living relative, because the Angel of Death coming to take the older relative might take the younger by mistake. Personally I doubt the Angel of Death is that careless, but why take chances?) Little Moishe is not so little, weighing maybe 250 pounds, while his father is weighing maybe half of that and really looking somewhat frail these days. It's something to see, I can tell you, the two of them on that big black machine: Motorcycle Moishe and Little Moishe, both in black leather jackets and black leather pants and with shiny black helmets on their heads—*nu*, at least they should be safe—roaring away, the father holding on for dear life to the son's waist, or as much of Little Moishe's substantial waist as his arms will fit around. And *oy*, with a noise that could wake the dead.

To tell the truth, every time I see and hear them ride off, I wonder whether they will return in one piece, because riding on one of those big machines looks to me about as safe as jumping off a cliff onto a pile of sharp rocks, shiny black helmet or no shiny black helmet.

Moishe is really a most pleasant man, always polite and with a smile for everyone. He lost his wife, Eva, to whom he was very devoted, about two years ago, and it took him a long time to get over her passing. But lately he has become again what you might call more social and has been trying hard to make new friends.

As I said, Moishe is a nice person, a *mensch*. He has just one little quirk. Well, maybe it's not so little. He still likes to dress like he is an "Angel from Hell," or whatever silly name they call themselves, even when he's not riding on his motorcycle. Is it not a bit silly for a man of maybe eighty years to walk around in a black leather jacket with knobbly silver things all over it and boots on his feet like he's in the army? *Es past vi a khazer oyringlekh*, as my mother would have said, it's like earrings on a pig. *Nu*, to each his own. At least he doesn't wear the helmet to dinner.

So here comes Moishe clomping along in his jacket and boots. When he sees me, he smiles like a man who has just been served a nice bowl of chicken soup. He stops and says to me, "Ida, just the person I wanted to see." I couldn't imagine why he wanted to see me, but soon I found out.

"Ida," says Moishe, "I want that you should come with me for a ride sometime on my motorcycle. You would have a good time, and we could get to know each other a little better."

Oy gevalt! Moishe did not speak many words in those two sentences, but what he did say, it set off several loud alarm bells in my head. First, I am being asked to go for a ride on that terrible machine of his, which I don't even like to be near when it's moving away from me. Second, I'm suddenly having a picture in my mind of sitting on that machine wearing one of those black leather jackets and shiny helmets. Can you imagine me, a proper lady of over seventy, in such a costume? Third, since there appear to be only two seats on the machine, he must be suggesting that it is he, and not Little Moishe, his son, who would be sitting on the front seat and driving. And this I'm sure he hasn't done in many years. Fourth, I would have to be wrapping my arms around Moishe's waist, like he has around his son's when he rides behind, which would be a most undignified thing for a lady of my age to be doing in public. And of course this leads to the last and most troubling thing about what Moishe is suggesting: that we should by doing this "get to know each other better."

****

Do not get me wrong. Even at my age, I'm not against having what people now refer to as a "relationship" with a man. I have been a widow for many years now, and I'm sure my dear husband, David, may he rest in peace, would not mind. In fact, such a thing is not uncommon here at the Home, at least among those of us who are still functioning properly in all the necessary ways, if you know what I mean.

No, the problem was not having a relationship, but only having one with Moishe Klein. He may be a very nice man and pleasant enough to talk to. In fact, I'm sure many of the widows at the Home would be most pleased to have such a relationship with him. But between Moishe and myself we have in common about as much as did Golda Meir and the pope. Well, perhaps a little more than that, but you understand. He is, to put it plainly, "not my type."

So when you put together that a man whom I have no interest in getting to know better is asking me to come and ride with him, on a machine of which I am terrified, while wearing a silly outfit I wouldn't want to be seen in and holding on to him like we're close friends, in order that we might become even closer friends, you can understand why those two short sentences of his sent a shiver right from my kop down my spine to my toes and back again. *Oy vey!*

****

As I was at a loss to know how to respond to Moishe's suggestion—I just stood there like a *shlemiel*—he spoke up again. "So how about it, Ida? What do you say?"

Now, what I should have said was, "Thank you for the invitation, Moishe, but I would rather not. It's nothing personal, but this isn't something I would enjoy doing." That is what I should have said. I'm certain that is what Mrs. K would have said. But Mrs. K thinks much more quickly on her feet than I do. The best I could come up with was, "Thank you, Moishe, I will have to think about it." And far from discouraging Moishe, this answer only gave him the idea I might actually be willing to ride on his motorcycle. He took my hand and squeezed it, said "Excellent," bowed slightly in the European manner, and then continued down the hall, leaving me to wonder into what kind of pickle I had just gotten myself.

Whatever kind of pickle it was, I was afraid it wouldn't be a good one.

****

Back in my room, I went over what had just happened and wondered how Mrs. K would have handled the situation with Moishe. Just before dinner, I stopped by her room to ask her.

"I wouldn't feel too bad about it, Ida," she said after I had told her about my strange encounter. "While Moishe might be a bit *meshugge*, he has always seemed like a *mensch*, really a good person who is maybe a *bissel* obsessed with his big toy."

"I agree, but that's not the point, Rose," I said, "although of course I would be more worried if he were a *momzer* instead of a *mensch*. No, it is that he seems to have some kind of 'relationship' in mind, and I have no desire at all to relate with him, whatever that might mean. Not to mention the part about riding with him on his machine."

Mrs. K just laughed. "You're taking this too seriously," she said. "My guess is that by tomorrow, if not already, Moishe will have forgotten all about his invitation. You'll see."

I didn't see, at least then. But a few days later, when

I again passed Moishe in the hallway, he simply smiled and nodded politely and passed by without a word. It seemed Mrs. K was right, as usual, and I had been taking Moishe—and perhaps myself—a little too seriously. I breathed a sigh of relief and went on my way.

Chapter Eight

The day after Fannie, Mrs. K, and I met with Dr. Menschyk (and I had my encounter with Motorcycle Moishe), Mrs. K received a telephone call from Fannie. She said she had spoken with Daniel and asked him if he would consent to an autopsy of his mother. Apparently he flatly refused, saying it was against *halacha*, or Jewish law. So Mrs. K and Dr. Menschyk had been right in assuming Daniel would not give his consent so easily. Fannie said she didn't try to argue with him, probably because she lacked the necessary information, and besides, since Mrs. K had offered to do the arguing for her, why should she bother?

Mrs. K having made the offer, then, she had to make good on it and try to convince Daniel to give his consent. So Mrs. K and I went to see Daniel. We had to visit him at his place of work, since of course he no longer would be coming to the Home to visit his mother, may she rest in peace.

Daniel was one of the senior pharmacists at a local Buy & Save Drug Mart, part of a big chain in the state, only a few miles from the Home. We had telephoned ahead and he said he could see us any time, as long as he was not in the middle of helping a customer.

"Before we visit Daniel," Mrs. K said as we waited for a taxi to arrive, "I think we should make a stop at Congregation Beth Shalom, which is the *shul* where

Daniel worships." Beth Shalom means "house of peace." *Shul* is just Yiddish for "school," and for Orthodox Jews calling it a school emphasizes that the synagogue is primarily a place to learn. So I was wondering what it was Mrs. K was wanting to learn at Daniel's *shul*.

"I'm thinking," she said when I asked, "that perhaps if we talk with his rabbi and can get the rabbi's approval, it will help to convince Daniel."

"And who is the rabbi at Beth Shalom? I know that Rabbi Goldstein, who was there for many years, retired recently, but I don't know who replaced him."

"I'm pretty sure he was replaced by a rabbi named Brown, or Brownstein, something like that. Unfortunately, I've never met him and have no idea how flexible he is on matters like this. As you know, there's a lot of—what would you call it?—a lot of wiggle room with regard to interpretations of the Torah. So we shall see."

The taxi dropped us off in front of a plain white building with "Congregation Beth Shalom" written across the entrance in big gold letters. We were fortunate that Rabbi Braunstein (Mrs. K had been close) was available to consult with us. We were ushered into his office by the receptionist. Rabbi Braunstein turned out to be a tall, slender man of maybe thirty-five or forty years, quite young compared to their former rabbi. We introduced ourselves, and when the rabbi asked what he could do for us, Mrs. K got right to the point.

"A good friend of ours, Daniel Gold, is one of your congregants." The rabbi nodded. "As you may know, his mother passed away recently. Her sister, Daniel's aunt, suspects there may have been…uh…what you might call foul play involved."

"You mean someone might have deliberately killed her?" the rabbi asked. He seemed somewhat surprised, as one would expect.

"Well, that's what his aunt suspects, yes." Mrs. K recounted briefly what Fannie had told us. The rabbi's jaw dropped a considerable distance as she was recounting.

"This sounds like it could be a serious matter," the rabbi said. "Has anyone gone to the police about it?"

"No, not yet," Mrs. K said. "It seemed best to first find out whether there was anything to go to them about. And to be honest, I doubt what we've told you would be enough for the police to start an investigation. So we thought first we should learn what Daniel's mother died of, and for that there must be an autopsy."

Rabbi Braunstein rubbed his chin and looked thoughtful.

"Yes, I see," he said. "And I take it you're aware of the prohibition against autopsies and have come to me to get my opinion, or maybe to get my blessing, so to speak. Is that right?"

This Rabbi Braunstein is pretty quick on the take-up, I thought. And he comes right to the point.

"Well, yes, that's right," Mrs. K said. "Do you think the circumstances warrant an exception from the usual prohibition?"

The rabbi did not answer right away, but he seemed to be turning this over in his mind. After a minute or two he shook his head a little and said, "This seems like something of a borderline case to me. That is, on the one hand, a murder investigation by the police is definitely a reason to relax the prohibition against autopsies, and in fact I doubt an objection on religious grounds would get very far if taken to court under such circumstances. But a murder investigation, so to speak, by a private person, even a close relative of the deceased, that's another thing entirely. I hate to say this, ladies, but it seems to me that it's one of those situations in which a person—Daniel in this case—would be justified in withholding his consent."

This, of course, was not what we wanted to hear. But Mrs. K is not one to take "no" for an answer when it's "yes" she wants to hear.

"I understand," she said. "But suppose we ask the question from the other side. Is this maybe an in-between situation in which Daniel would also be justified in giving his consent? Is it maybe so in-between that either way would not be violating *halacha*?"

Again, the rabbi took his time thinking. When he answered he clearly was choosing his words carefully.

"Hmm, I suppose you have a point there, Mrs. Kaplan. I did say it was a borderline case, and as such I do think Daniel could be...could be justified in deciding either way, although on balance I still have to come down more on the side of no autopsy." He paused before continuing, "Now, if you'd like me to do some research and see if this question has been decided before..."

Mrs. K rose and said quickly, "No, I don't think that will be necessary, but I thank you very much for offering..."

"Or," he interrupted, "we could gather some members of the community and convene a *beit din*, and it could decide the matter..."

"No, no, I wouldn't think of making such a big deal of this. And there really isn't time to go through such a process." A *beit din* (which means "house of judgment") is a Jewish court. It goes back to Biblical times, and today in America it usually is used only to settle a dispute within the Jewish community. Three members of the community are selected to sit in judgment. Clearly Mrs. K felt she had gotten as good an answer already as she was liable to get and didn't want to take a chance on what some strangers might decide.

We both thanked Rabbi Braunstein for his time and his advice. He seemed a *bissel* amused by our hasty exit, and I'm sure he understood exactly why Mrs. K was content to take what she had and run. Like I said, he's a sharp one, that Braunstein, and he doesn't miss much.

The receptionist called for us another taxi, and while we waited for it outside, Mrs. K said, "So, Ida. What did you think of Rabbi Braunstein?"

"That man has *saichel*," I said. "Common sense. He knew what you needed to hear, but he also knew what he had to say. He walked this tightrope very well, I thought."

"So did I," replied Mrs. K. "It is a wise man who knows when to speak, when not to speak, and also when to do both at the same time."

We continued by taxi to Daniel's place of work, the Buy & Save Drug Mart on Twelfth Street. It's a big place, with a parking lot for maybe a hundred cars all around it, like a black moat with white stripes and a few colored boats floating here and there. As soon as we got near the glass doors that said "Entrance," they swooshed open, with a sound like a large person taking a deep breath, and we walked in. They call it a "drugstore," but in most of it they sell no drugs, but everything else from toys to televisions. Only a small part in the back is for buying drugs. When I was younger, the only drugstore we went to had an orange and blue sign on the outside that said "Rexall," and inside the only things they sold other than actual drugs were maybe corn plasters and Epsom salts. Maybe also some Juicy Fruit gum and Life Savers.

The pharmacy part of the store was against the back wall, and we made our way there, passing by many things—like bags of salted snacks and sweet drinks, even liquor—that, if a person ate or used a lot of them, would make it much more likely they would need to buy medicines at the pharmacy. Maybe that's why these "drugstores" sell them!

Daniel was busy with preparing some potion or other for a customer, so we sat down on the chairs set aside for people waiting for their prescriptions. The one I was sitting on had a little plastic switch on it. It was turned off, but I wondered what it was for, so I pushed it to "on." Immediately my seat—and I do mean both the chair and my *tuchis*—began to vibrate. It was most embarrassing, especially because I gave a little shriek— only a little one, but enough for Mrs. K to look over and see me squirming and shaking like I had *shpilkes*, pins and needles—you know, ants in the pants. She looked alarmed.

"Ida, is something the matter? What's wrong?"

"No, nothing is wrong, it's just…" I managed to say, although my voice went up and down every time I did. I was fumbling for the switch to turn the vibrations off, but I couldn't find it.

Fortunately, Mrs. K figured out what was happening and she reached over and turned off the machine. What a relief! I'm surprised they're allowed to sell these machines, much less inflict them on unsuspecting customers. I quickly moved to the next chair.

After a few more minutes—during which I recovered my dignity and we had a chance to examine closely several magazines and a special on toilet paper—Daniel came out from behind the counter and greeted us.

"Hello, Rose, Ida." He gave us each a little hug. "It's nice to see you again. I've missed our little chats when I was at the Home. So what can I do for you? Fill a prescription?" He sat down next to us, in the chair with the tricky switch. I'm sure he knew enough not to press it, though.

Mrs. K first said how sorry we were about his mother's passing, although of course we had said this already at the funeral. He thanked us and asked after our health, which for a pharmacist might be a business as well as a personal question. We assured him we were in good health, except for my bursitis and a few minor aches and pains. I'm not sure he really wanted to know.

"So, Daniel, how is it to work in this big, fancy store?"

Daniel rolled his eyes and said, his voice lowered a bit, "To be honest, Rose, it's not like when I was working at the Fourteenth Street Pharmacy." This was a small, family-owned drugstore where Daniel worked before they closed—they couldn't compete with the big chain—and he moved to Buy & Save.

"No? Is that because it's such a large place?"

"Well, it's that, but also it's the whole experience. When I was at Fourteenth Street, I knew everyone and everyone knew me. I mean, the people I worked with had been there for many years, like I had, and most of the customers were from that neighborhood and I knew them by name. It was like we were all family, and I was in the position of helping them to get well."

"And it's not like that here?"

Glancing around first, Daniel said, "I'm afraid not. First of all, we serve a much bigger area, not just a neighborhood, so a lot of the people we see have never been in before, or they go to whatever branch is handy when they need a prescription filled. They might come in here once or twice a year. And even with people who come in regularly, we're under pressure to get prescriptions out as fast as possible, so for the most part they hire clerks to deal with the public—to take in the prescriptions and deliver them when they're filled—and about the only time we pharmacists talk with customers is when we're called out to make sure that someone taking a medicine for the first time knows what it is and how to take it. There's not much time or opportunity to really become acquainted, or talk with them if we already know them."

"But here you're talking nicely with us, aren't you?"

"Of course, but I've had to make this my coffee break; otherwise I couldn't take so much time with one customer."

"I see," Mrs. K said. She sounded a little concerned, as a mother might be if her son was having difficulty at work. "So if you aren't happy, are you planning to continue working here?"

Daniel lowered his voice further and said to us, "As a matter of fact, I'm not. Can I tell you something in confidence?"

"Certainly," Mrs. K said.

"Well, I guess it's sort of an 'every cloud has a silver lining' thing. While my mother's passing was a very sad thing, it was not really unexpected given her age and her illness. She died peacefully, and what more can you ask? When it's a person's time, it's their time; it's all in the hands of *Hashem*." (*Hashem* just means "the name," and it's how many religious Jews refer to God.) "And as a result, I'm expecting to receive an inheritance that should allow me to quit this job and do whatever I want. It's not the way you want to become wealthy, of course, but it will be a great help to me and my family. And that's what my mother wanted."

"And how do you know this inheritance is coming to you?"

"Well, it's not official yet, but to be honest, I did help my mother to draw up her will. She didn't trust anyone else, even her lawyer. So I know there was a large gift to me. She wanted her estate divided half to me and the other half split between Fred Herrington and the Home. But I probably shouldn't be telling you this until the will is official. And to be honest, I haven't yet seen the will—I never had a copy. I think the police have it, but if so, it should be in her lawyer's hands any time now."

"And who is this Fred Herrington, that he should be getting a quarter of the estate?" I asked.

Daniel looked surprised. "I'm sorry, I assumed you knew. After my dad died, maybe a year later my mother met this fellow Fred Herrington. He was somewhat younger than her, but they seemed to hit it off. They ended up living together for about four years, including the time when my mother made the will I'm telling you about. I don't think they ever actually married."

Mrs. K clicked her tongue. "Who knew?"

Mrs. K and I certainly didn't. I doubt even nosy Mrs. Bissela did.

"How did you feel about this, as Vera's son?" Mrs. K asked.

"Well, I guess I had mixed feelings. On the one hand, he seemed to make my mother happy, which was often a pretty good trick, and I appreciated that. On the other, I couldn't help worrying that he was just after her money."

"Did you suggest this when your mother said she wanted him in her will?"

Daniel laughed. "I did kind of hint at it, maybe a bit more than hint, but you knew my mother, and you know that when she decided to do something, you didn't easily talk her out of it. In fact, if you tried, she just might get even more determined."

I could believe that.

"So what happened to Mr. Herrington?"

"Actually, I'm not sure. At that time my mother wasn't living very close to me and I only saw her occasionally, and Herrington and I didn't really get along that well. Then he kind of disappeared from the scene, and when I asked my mother about it, she never gave me a straight answer. I assume they had a falling out of some kind and he just left. I know my mother wasn't the easiest person to live with, and as I recall he was kind of a milquetoast, sort of meek and timid. Or maybe she kicked him out for some reason. Anyway, soon after that she moved to the Home."

"And did she change her will after she moved?"

Daniel thought about this. "I really don't know. She never asked me to help her with it again. I just assume ol' Fred is still due to get that money. But if so, there's plenty to go around."

"This will, you didn't sign it as a witness, did you?"

Mrs. K asked, sounding a bit alarmed. "I know that would mean you couldn't take the money."

Daniel laughed. "No, no. I knew that. No, my mother and I discussed what she wanted, and then we had a lawyer actually draw up the will and he signed it as a witness, together with a couple of secretaries in his office. So that's how I know what it said. But I'm running out of time on my break here, and I assume you wanted to see me about more than how I like my job. What was it?"

This was going to be awkward for us, as you can imagine. Here Daniel is making known how his mother's death, while of course heartbreaking, was perfectly natural, and it's even a financial benefit to him and his family. And now we must tell him it's maybe not so simple.

Mrs. K cleared her throat and plunged in. "I believe your aunt Frances already may have asked you, but there seems to be some question from exactly what your mother died. So Frances would like that there should be an autopsy." She obviously didn't want to upset him with a suggestion about Vera being murdered, if it was not absolutely necessary.

Daniel looked slightly distressed by the question and didn't answer right away. But after a few seconds, he said, "As you probably know, Rose, it's against Jewish law to perform an autopsy. So like I told Aunt Frances, I wouldn't be able to agree to that. I'm sorry."

Unfortunately, then, we had to give Daniel more details as to why we were asking. Mrs. K told him what Fannie had said, in a much abbreviated version, of course.

If Daniel looked slightly distressed before, he turned

very pale at hearing this new information. And who could blame him?

It took him a minute before he recovered a bit and asked, "Did you...did you say that you ... that Aunt Frances and you...think my mother was...was murdered?" He put his hand on his forehead, as if trying to understand. I can just imagine how I would have felt if someone had told me, after my mother or father had just passed away, that they might have been murdered. *Oy vey*, I probably would have fainted!

Mrs. K glanced at me sideways, then she patted Daniel's hand and said to him, "No, Daniel, not exactly. All we are saying is that your mother may have said something to your aunt that makes us all wonder whether such an awful thing is just possible. I personally believe your mother died of perfectly natural causes, and Ida here does also. Of course, what we believe or don't believe is not important, as we are not your family; but your aunt seems to be...to be uncertain, and she very much wants to have this question put to rest."

"And that's why she wants an autopsy? To show that my mother was murdered?" Daniel's voice was rising; clearly he didn't like this idea.

"No, Daniel dear, not to show she was murdered, but to show she was not. Just, as I say, to put the matter to rest, especially in her mind. So she should not forever wonder about it. I mean, on the off chance there was some...some foul play, as they say, would you not want to know that, and to find the person responsible?"

Daniel shook his head slowly. "No. I mean yes, I would want to find the person responsible, if such a thing had happened; but no, I don't believe any such thing did happen, and something a very sick woman might at some time have said doesn't seem like a good enough reason to violate my mother's body and disturb her final resting place in order to find out. And in any event, as I've already said, an autopsy is contrary to Jewish law, so that should end the matter."

He then took a breath after this long speech and said, "I'm sorry. I know you're just trying to help and have my—and my mother's—best interests at heart. But I hope you understand why I can't agree to an autopsy."

Mrs. K took Daniel's hand and looked at him kindly, like a mother at her son.

"That is your right, of course," she said softly. "And I understand about *halacha*. But let me try just once more to convince you. First, your aunt Frances is a very kind person and she clearly loved your mother, her sister, from all we have seen while she has been living at the Home. I'm sure you can understand how she must feel, having been told what she was told. It would be a real kindness to relieve her mind, even at the expense of disturbing your dear mother's rest."

Daniel looked down and was silent for a while before saying, "Yes, I understand, and I'd like to help Aunt Frances. But remember it would still be prohibited by Jewish law. I can't get around that." He clearly considered that this point should end the discussion. But Mrs. K, as usual, had anticipated this.

"Yes, there is still *halacha*. But perhaps we have resolved this remaining obstacle." I admired how Mrs. K had made it as if Daniel had said he would allow the autopsy if only *halacha* permitted it, which is not exactly what he said and probably not what he meant. And of course on this question, she was already prepared.

"Ida and I stopped in to see Rabbi Braunstein before

coming here. We explained the situation as we have explained it to you and asked whether it is true that under the circumstances Jewish law would prevent you from permitting the autopsy."

Daniel looked a bit surprised at this information and waited to hear what his rabbi had said. He probably realized Mrs. K would not have brought it up if it supported his position.

"Of course," Mrs. K went on, "it's not a simple question. But what question of *halacha* is? Scholars spend their entire lives arguing over how to interpret a word or two in the Torah. But on one thing he was clear: If the question is whether, under the circumstances we have discussed, you would be justified in permitting an autopsy, his answer was yes." This was, of course, literally true. That Daniel would also have been justified in doing the opposite, and that the rabbi himself believed denial of the autopsy was the stronger case, she neglected to mention. But that was not the question, was it?

Daniel closed his eyes and put his head between his hands, shaking his head slightly back and forth, as if trying to make sense of all of this information and emotion that was running around inside. I felt sorry for him and wished Mrs. K and I had never become involved in this sad story. I especially wished Mrs. K had not agreed to take Fannie's side, it being so unlikely Vera had died from anything except her illness.

Finally Daniel looked up at us and said very softly, "I have to go back to work now, and I can't think straight about what you've told me. I'll think about it tonight and let you—let Aunt Frances, that is—know in the morning. Is that okay?"

Mrs. K put her arm around Daniel's shoulders and

said kindly, "Of course. This is a difficult decision even in the best of circumstances. Take whatever time you need to, and let your aunt know. However you decide, I'm sure you will be doing what you believe best. That is all anyone can ask."

She gave him a pat on the arm as she and I rose to leave. He got up also and returned to his work.

But clearly he would not have his mind on his work this afternoon.

It might be best, I thought, for the rest of the day not to order from him a prescription.

****

The next day, as Mrs. K and I were sipping our morning tea in the lounge, Fannie came over looking excited. She sat down next to us and said, "I just received a telephone call from Daniel. He said he had spoken with you and had decided to allow the autopsy. I'm so relieved."

Mrs. K took her hand and said, "We're pleased too, Ida and I, because it's best for everyone that this matter be resolved one way or the other. And it should be resolved before anyone else learns of what your sister told you. Can you imagine the talk around the Home, even if there is nothing suspicious found?"

"Mrs. Bissela would have a field day, wouldn't she?" I said.

Mrs. K just rolled her eyes.

"So what is your next step?" Mrs. K asked Fannie.

"Well, I'll get in touch with Dr. Menschyk, of course, and get the ball rolling so we can put this awful matter behind us as soon as possible."

"Fine. Keep me and Ida informed. Obviously, we are quite interested to find out the results of the autopsy.

Of course, we all hope they are negative, and that your sister died of perfectly natural causes."

"Of course," replied Fannie with a kind of sad smile, and she stood up and walked away.

Mrs. K and I watched her go and could not help but feel sorry for her.

"Poor Fannie," Mrs. K said as we returned to our tea. "If the results of the autopsy are negative, she has stirred up such a fuss for nothing. But if they indicate murder, what she will have stirred up will be far worse than a fuss."

"Yes," I agreed. "It will be only the beginning of a very long ordeal. From which no one comes out happy."

Chapter Nine

It apparently takes a while for all the paperwork needed for an autopsy, and then of course to perform it and analyze the results. So it was not until several days later that there was the next development.

Mrs. K and I were sitting in the lounge as usual after breakfast, reading our magazines, when she nudges me and says in a surprised tone, "Ida, isn't that the policeman Corcoran who just came in the door, together with that *shlumper* Jenkins?"

"You mean the one who looks like that Inspector Dalgleish from television?"

"Yes, and the one who looks like the other television detective Columbo, only much messier. I wonder what they're doing here this time."

I should mention for those who might have missed it, there was an earlier incident here at the Home involving a resident who died while eating Mrs. K's excellent matzoh ball soup—it is too complicated to explain, you should read the story—and these were the two detectives who investigated the case. I know that Corcoran, who is clearly the brains of the pair—not to mention the looks—was quite impressed with Mrs. K's ability to figure out the solution to that case.

"Have you talked with this Corcoran since he was last here on that case involving your soup?" I asked.

"Yes. Do you remember my telling you he had

called me about a month later and invited me to lunch? I think you were away visiting your sister at the time."

"That's right. And as I recall, you said you and he had a nice chat."

"He's really a very charming young man, you know. He not only thanked me for helping him avoid a bad mistake, but he said he might someday call on me again, should the need arise. That was very nice of him, and I assumed he was just being polite, but now here he is, and I wonder what it's all about."

What it was about we learned later in the day from, who else? From Mrs. Bissela, the resident *yenta*. How she manages to find out what other people cannot, and so quickly, is a complete mystery to me, but she obviously has her sources.

Mrs. K and I were talking with Isaac Taubman in the lobby of the Home when Mrs. Bissela comes up behind us and taps Mrs. K on the shoulder. When Mrs. K turned around, Mrs. Bissela whispered something in her ear. Mrs. K looked a bit annoyed, but she turned back to us and said, "Pardon us for a minute, Isaac. Apparently Hannah has something important she wants to tell us and she says it cannot wait."

Taubman is always the gentleman. "Of course, Rose," he said. "I was just on my way out for a walk anyway, so we can talk later."

We thanked him and then made our way to the lounge. We poured ourselves some tea and sat down next to Mrs. Bissela, who I could tell was very anxious to say something. As soon as we were seated, she looked at Mrs. K and said, "I know you and Ida are very interested in how Vera Gold died, may she rest in peace. You and Ida and of course her sister, Fannie."

I have no idea how Hannah learned of this, or how she learns of anything for that matter, but we couldn't deny it, could we?

"Well, I've heard that a couple of police detectives came to visit Pupik this morning, and apparently they told him that Vera did not die from her disease, but somebody, shall we say, hurried her along."

I was shocked, of course, having poo-pooed the idea from the beginning, and I'm sure Mrs. K was surprised as well, although if so she didn't reveal it in her face. She calmly asked, "You mean she was murdered?" I chimed in with "How? Why? By whom?"

Unfortunately, Mrs. Bissela didn't have any of these answers. All she knew, she said, was that it was now a police matter. And that Pupik was not at all pleased about it. He is not pleased about almost anything, but at least here I don't blame him.

We thanked Mrs. Bissela for the information.

"Well, I thought you two would like to know," she said. "I assume we shall all learn more about it soon." What she meant was that she would find a way to learn more, and then we would all know.

We talked a few more minutes, but there was no more information to be had, and Mrs. Bissela went on her way.

Mrs. K and I just looked at each other for a minute after Mrs. Bissela had left, absorbing the news. Then something occurred to me.

"So do you think Fannie knows this already?"

Mrs. K laughed. "Now, Ida, do you think if Hannah Bissela went to the trouble of telling this to me, someone who is only very indirectly involved, that she didn't already tell Vera's sister, who got the feathers flying in the first place?"

I had to admit this was extremely unlikely.

"Actually," Mrs. K went on, "since it was Fannie who arranged for the autopsy, she probably knew from Menschyk or someone else even before Hannah told her. In any case, I wouldn't be surprised if we were to hear from Fannie very shortly."

But as it happened, it wasn't Fannie we next heard from, but the policeman Corcoran, of whom I've already spoken. In fact, he was at that moment making his way across the lounge toward where we were sitting. Jenkins was trailing after him, looking dyspeptic as usual whenever we have seen him. I would like to think that by him it's just a permanent condition and not anything personal about Mrs. K and myself.

"Hello, ladies. It's been a while," Corcoran said when he arrived by us. He smiled warmly and offered his hand, and we each shook it. Jenkins arrived a few seconds later. No hand, just a nod. A real sourpuss is that Jenkins.

The two policemen sat on a sofa opposite us. Even sitting it was quite a contrast between them: Slender and handsome Corcoran, with his dark hair combed back and thin moustache, wearing a nice pressed pinstripe suit; and pudgy and *shlumpy* (unkempt) Jenkins, his thinning hair combed to one side and his wrinkled suit sitting on him like it couldn't quite find a comfortable place to lie down.

Jenkins took out a notebook and pen. What is it they say in the TV shows when one is talking with a policeman? Anything we say may be taken down and used in evidence against us? I was very much hoping we weren't being suspected of something!

Corcoran looked over at Jenkins and gestured he should put the notebook away. Jenkins did, but he didn't look happy about it.

We talked for a few minutes about things that had happened since that other case I mentioned had ended. Corcoran said he is now "Inspector," which I assume is a promotion from whatever he was before. Eventually he got around to why he was visiting.

"As much as I enjoy chatting with you ladies, you've probably guessed that I'm actually here on business."

We nodded.

"So I'll come right to the point. As you doubtless know, Vera Gold, one of the residents here, passed away last week."

Again we nodded. Neither of us was surprised that Vera was the reason the detectives were here.

"Well, it turns out that her death was not from natural causes, as had been assumed. Either by accident or otherwise, Mrs. Gold apparently died from the medications she had taken."

Mrs. K and I stared at each other, both of us trying to understand just what Inspector Corcoran was saying. He had not said she was murdered; not in so many words, at least. Just that it was not "natural causes." It could have been an accident. Mrs. Bissela might have gotten the story wrong.

"Now, the reason I'm telling you this," Corcoran went on, "is that I've already spoken briefly with Mrs. Kleinberg, Mrs. Gold's sister, and as I understand it, she was the one who first raised the possibility that her sister's death was not—not as it appeared, and she told you this. You then were instrumental in persuading Mrs.

Gold's son, Daniel, to permit an autopsy and, well, here we are. Is that correct?"

Both of us nodded that it was.

"Right. That being the case, I can speak freely with you about the matter, as you are, shall we say, principals in the story so far."

I was not sure I wanted to be a "principal" in a murder, if that is what it was, but Corcoran was smiling and it didn't appear this meant anything bad.

"Besides," Corcoran continued, turning toward Mrs. K, "I find it both pleasant and very informative to talk with you, Mrs. Kaplan. Who better to consult about this little drama and the various characters in it? And you too, of course, Mrs. Berkowitz," he added, looking then at me, "if that's okay with you both." It was nice he wanted not to leave me out, although I knew it was mostly Mrs. K he wanted to consult. So would I.

"Yes, certainly, we'll be glad to help any way we can," Mrs. K said. "Won't we, Ida?"

I nodded. "Yes, of course," I said. *Nu*, as long as I am not being suspected of anything, and neither is Mrs. K, the policemen can ask me anything they want. In fact, it might turn out to be much more exciting than reading about it in the newspaper later.

"Good," Corcoran said. "Now you'll understand that whatever we discuss will be in strict confidence. I and Sergeant Jenkins here will not repeat what you tell us to anyone who doesn't have to know, and we ask that you do the same." He then added with a little laugh, "I'm aware things get around a place like this very fast, just like they do in any close community. Let's see if we can cut this particular discussion off at the source."

We both nodded. "Does that include Fannie…I

mean Mrs. Kleinberg?" Mrs. K asked. "After all, she's the one who brought us into this in the first place."

"Yes, I know. Let's just say use your judgment. As I said, let's not discuss this with anyone who doesn't need to know. And I might add that I'll try not to tell you anything you don't need to know. Of course what Mrs. Kleinberg already knows is no problem. And she knows everything I've already told you. But that's all we said to her."

That seemed clear enough.

"Could I ask," Mrs. K said, "what medicine it was that caused Vera's—Mrs. Gold's—death?"

"I don't see any harm in that, although again let's keep this kind of detail just between us for now. It's actually a bit strange. You may or may not have been aware that Mrs. Gold was being treated for, among other things, a mild case of schizophrenia."

"We did know she had some…some mental issues," Mrs. K said.

"Right. For that she was taking a drug called"—and here he took out his own notebook and flipped through the pages until he found what he wanted—"called ziprasidone. Perfectly normal, considered safe. Took it every evening. And the autopsy revealed that ziprasidone was indeed in her system when she died."

Now if Corcoran had said she was taking aspirin, I would have had no problem. But although I am writing here the name of the medicine as if I right away understood, the truth is that at the time Inspector Corcoran said the name, it was, as they say, Greek to me. Maybe even Sanskrit. I later had him write it down for me so I could include it here.

"The problem arose," he continued, "when

somehow—we don't yet know how, of course—Mrs. Gold also ingested another drug, called"—and again he looked at his notebook—sibutramine, which had not been prescribed for her. In fact, it hasn't been prescribed for anyone for some time, as it was taken off the market a few years ago."

"Taken off the market?" said Mrs. K. "Why was that?"

"I'm not entirely sure, but apparently there were health risks involved."

"What was it a medicine for?" I asked.

"It was an appetite suppressant, some kind of a diet pill."

"And why would a person like Vera, who was maybe the last person here who needed a diet pill, have taken such a medicine?" Mrs. K asked.

"Exactly," said Corcoran. "And even if she wanted to lose weight, how and why did she take a pill that's been off the market for so long? Where, or from whom, did she even get it?"

"Perhaps she used to be overweight, and that's when she got those pills," I said.

"Perhaps," Corcoran said, "but that still wouldn't explain her taking them now."

"No," I agreed. "It's a mystery."

"Yes, but we'll leave that to the medical folks for now."

"So how can we help you?" Mrs. K asked.

"Well, first I'd appreciate it if you would take me through your discussion with Mrs. Kleinberg, from the time she approached you about her sister's death."

"Certainly," Mrs. K answered, as Jenkins again took out his notebook and pen. This time Corcoran didn't try to discourage him. "Ida, you be sure to say if I leave anything out or you disagree with something." I nodded.

Mrs. K then told the policemen what Fannie had said about Vera being afraid of being poisoned, our visit with Dr. Menschyk, his suggesting an autopsy would be the only way to be absolutely certain, Daniel's reluctance to permit one, and her helping to convince Daniel to allow it. She left out that Mrs. Bissela had told her the results before he had; this he didn't need to know.

Both Corcoran and Jenkins took notes while Mrs. K was telling, Corcoran making little "hmm" and "I see" noises from time to time. When she had finished, he asked the same question Mrs. K had asked Fannie: "Did Mrs. Kleinberg say whether her sister had mentioned that she suspected anyone in particular of trying to poison her?"

Mrs. K shook her head. "I asked her that and she said no. That is, she didn't mention a name, but…" She looked over at me and said, "Ida, didn't she say something like Vera did suspect someone but didn't want to say who?"

"Yes," I said. "I think she said it seemed to be upsetting her, who it was she suspected."

Just then Jenkins spoke up for the first time. "I'd think it'd be upsetting that anyone was trying to poison you," he said.

"Yes," said Mrs. K, "but I had the impression from what Fannie—Mrs. Kleinberg—said that there was something about who it was that made her not want to say the name if she was not absolutely sure."

"Well," said Corcoran, flipping back a few pages in his notebook, "that pretty much jibes with what Mrs. Kleinberg told us when we spoke with her. Thank you, ladies. It's very helpful to get your perspective. Now, stepping aside from the facts about Mrs. Gold's death for a moment—and this is where I think you can especially be of service in our preliminary investigation—I wonder if you wouldn't mind giving us a brief rundown on what you might call the cast of characters here."

"You mean you want to know about everyone at the Home?" Mrs. K said. "That would take quite a while…"

"No, no. I'm sorry. What I meant was could you tell us what you know about—what your impressions are—about the few people directly involved in the case, at least so far. That would include…" and he again flipped around in his notebook, glancing also over at the one Jenkins was holding, "…Mrs. Gold, of course, as well as Mrs. Kleinberg, Mrs. Gold's son, Daniel, and…well, and anyone who comes to mind who might possibly have had a reason to harm Mrs. Gold."

"You mean any possible suspects?" Mrs. K asked. The tone of her voice had now changed a little. I could tell that she was becoming more enthusiastic. Being asked by Inspector Corcoran to suggest who had a motive to kill Vera meant she was playing a role in the investigation, almost an official role. Her Sherlock Holmes instincts—as I said, she's a great fan of his— were waking up. It's like I've seen on television that when the bugle is blown at a fox hunt, the hounds that have been acting lazy and uninterested suddenly perk up their ears and are ready to chase down the poor fox. Mrs. K's ears were definitely perking. She was ready for the chase.

"Well, you could put it that way," Corcoran said. "Now please understand that at this time, we don't know whether Mrs. Gold's death was an accident or intentional, just that it was not what you'd call natural. And I wouldn't exactly say anyone with a grudge against Mrs. Gold was automatically a 'suspect.' But yes, if you know of people who might have had such a motive, I'd appreciate that information, so we could follow it up. Of course, no one will know you mentioned them to us."

"And no one will get in trouble just because I mention them to you?"

"Don't worry about that, Mrs. Kaplan. We realize many people might have disliked Mrs. Gold for any number of reasons, none of which necessarily makes them a suspect. But we do have to check them out, so to speak."

Mrs. K seemed satisfied. "I'm sure Ida and I would be pleased to be of help. In fact, we could give you a little list right now, because unfortunately Mrs. Gold was not what you would call the most popular resident here." Mrs. K is so good at the understatement. "But we will do a little snooping around to see if we can add anyone else to the list."

Corcoran laughed. "I'm sure you will, and that's fine. But if you can give us some information now, we can get started checking it out."

So Mrs. K and I told the policemen what we knew about Vera, Daniel, and Fannie, while Jenkins took notes furiously, almost never looking up from his notebook. Mrs. K asked Corcoran for a little more time to consider the other persons, those who might be suspects.

"Of course," he answered. "We'll be conducting our investigation just as we ordinarily would, and your information will just give us additional insights that we might not otherwise learn." He then thanked us, giving both of us a nice warm smile—which made up for the sour expression still on Jenkins's face, although he did nod to us as he turned to go—and left the lounge.

Mrs. K and I looked at each other in silence for a minute. Then she said, "Ida, as Mr. Sherlock Holmes would say, 'the game, it is afoot.'"

I don't know about her feet, but it was pretty clear that all Mrs. K needed now was Mr. Holmes's funny hat and the fancy pipe.

And maybe a tweed suit? Or is that Miss Marple who wears one of those?

Chapter Ten

We decided that a discussion such as we were going
to have regarding possible murder suspects among our
friends and fellow residents was best held somewhere
other than where we all live, not to mention where Mrs.
Bissela is always lurking. So we caught the afternoon
shuttle that takes us downtown, where is our favorite
place to have tea and to *shmooze*, the Garden Gate Café.

"Where are you ladies headed?" Andy, the shuttle
bus driver, asked as we climbed up the steps and onto the
bus. "Doing a little shopping?"

"Not exactly," I said. "Could you drop us off near
the Garden Gate Café, please? We are going for tea."

"You're sure you wouldn't rather be dropped off at
Mickey's Tavern for a couple of beers?" Andy said,
smiling. He likes to *kibitz*, that Andy.

I laughed, and not just because Andy made a joke,
but because it made in my mind such a picture. I could
see the two of us perched like large animals on high bar
stools, holding glasses of beer and *fressing* peanuts from
a dish on the bar. *Oy*, there is more chance of finding a
pig at the seder table!

Anyway, we found our seats and, after a few other
residents had come aboard, Andy closed the doors and
we were on our way.

As we rode, I asked Mrs. K whether she had as yet
thought of a way to help Sol Lipman deal with Lily's

mother.

"Not entirely," she said. "What I know is that it must be done in such a way that Lily's mother leaves their apartment voluntarily. She must want to leave, and Lily must not have the feeling that Sol is kicking her out. Otherwise, there will be more trouble between them, if not now then the next time they have an argument, which knowing them would be very soon. Lily should not be accusing Sol of treating her mother badly."

"You're right, of course," I said. "So how will you manage that trick?"

Just then Andy put the brakes on quite suddenly, as some *shlemiel*, probably *shikker*—a fool having too much to drink—swerved in front of the bus. We all fell forward and had to grab onto a rail, or onto each other, to keep from falling onto the floor. Andy always reserves these rare occasions to demonstrate to us the wide range of his vocabulary, and who can blame him? Someone on the bus waved their fist and shouted "A *khalerye*" (it is what Sol should not have said to Lily's mother), and there were a few other Yiddish curses I will not repeat. If only Andy knew a little Yiddish, he would have so many more insults to choose from.

We settled ourselves back into our seats, but our talk now turned to drunken drivers and what should be done to them, and I had to postpone finding out how Lily's mother would be made to leave.

****

Andy dropped us off as close to the Garden Gate Café as he could manage, and we had about two blocks to walk. We didn't mind, as it was a pleasant day, not too warm or too cold, and a little walk does us good. We were looking forward to our tea and a nice bagel with a *shmear—Nu*, the cream cheese is not good for us, but who can resist?—when we arrived at the café and had a surprise. There was a sign on the window of the front door that said in big red letters, "Closed for remodeling. We reopen next week. Thank you for your patience."

Oy gevalt, what to do now? Andy would not be back to pick us up for at least an hour, so time was on our hands.

"Well, Ida," Mrs. K said, "what do you think we should do?"

"We could just look around, I suppose, shop in the windows ."

That didn't appeal to Mrs. K, and to be honest it didn't to me either. I know it's something people do, but why waste a lot of time looking at things one has no intention of buying?

"Perhaps then we could find another tea shop nearby," I suggested.

"Yes, that would be best. But it's been so long since we went anywhere but the Garden Gate, I have no idea what else there is around here."

We began looking around us. Something caught my eye.

"Look across the street," I said. "It looks like a new café has just opened. I can't read the name from here, but there's a big sign saying 'Grand Opening,' and it certainly looks like it might be a restaurant."

Mrs. K looked where I was pointing and said, "You might be right, Ida. Let's cross over and take a closer look."

We walked to the corner and waited for the light to be green, then made our way across the busy street. The closer we came, the better we could see what kind of place it was that was having such a grand opening. And sure enough, it was a restaurant of some kind, because there were tables and chairs out on the sidewalk with big umbrellas over them, and on the door was a very ornate sign with curly gold letters saying, "The Purple Rose."

"Look," I said to Mrs. K, "it's even your name on the door."

She laughed and said, "Then of course we must go in."

We opened the polished wood door and stepped inside. "I think this is a much fancier place than the Garden Gate Café," I said. "Look at the drapes and the white table cloths."

"Fancy shmancy. As long as they serve a cup of tea, who cares?"

A sign on a wooden stand said, "Please seat yourself." It was a large room, with shiny wood panels on the walls and a red carpet on the floor. There was a long bar at the front and maybe a dozen tables, about half of which were already taken. We found a nice table near a window and, as the sign said, we seated ourselves.

"I wonder why we haven't heard about this new restaurant opening," I said. "Usually they make quite a hoo-hah about such things."

"You're right," Mrs. K said. "We must have missed whatever announcement they made, and maybe it's too new to have been reviewed in the newspaper." Actually, neither of us always reads the local newspaper, the Citizen, as there is usually just bad news we are better off not knowing about. But then we miss local happenings like this new restaurant opening.

Just then a waiter came over and handed us menus. They were crisp and new, just like the restaurant, as if they had hardly yet been opened. Maybe we were the first to use them. The liquid selections were mostly alcoholic drinks, but tea was mentioned and that is all we wanted. That and maybe a *nosh*, a snack, to go with it.

The waiter was certainly different from what we were used to at the Garden Gate. There we usually were waited on by a young blond girl or an older lady with curly brown hair who has been there as long as we've been visiting. The waiter who brought the menus was a very thin young man of maybe twenty with what you might call soft features and dark hair combed straight back. He was wearing a shirt made of some shiny material in many colors, with a black apron tied to his waist. For some reason the impression I got was that there was something a little different about him, but I couldn't say what.

"My name is Lawrence and I'll be your server," he said in a soft, pleasant voice. "May I get you ladies something to drink before you order?" I had forgotten that no one is a waiter anymore; they are all "servers." Pardon me, but to me they are still waiters and waitresses.

"What kind of tea do you have?" Mrs. K asked. "That is really all we want, and maybe a toasted bagel?"

The waiter now looked just a *bissel* confused. He swallowed and said, "I'm sorry, but we just opened yesterday and this is the first time I've been asked about tea. Of course we have tea, but I'm not sure what kind. And a bagel...I don't know about that either. I'll just go and check and be right back." He walked away looking somewhat embarrassed, but it's understandable that in a new restaurant it will take some time before everyone knows everything about the menu, and we didn't mind that he went to ask. Meanwhile I got out a pad and pencil from my purse and pulled my chair closer to Mrs. K's so we could speak privately.

"While we are waiting," I said, "let's begin to consider what the policeman Corcoran asked."

"That's a good idea, Ida. So who is it that particularly disliked Vera? At least disliked her more than everyone else did? I don't think she was really liked by anyone, except perhaps her son and her sister. But most of us just ignored her. Who might want to do more than that?"

"Well, we could begin with Rena Shapiro," I said.

"Yes," Mrs. K said, "I have never seen her so angry as when Vera told Pupik about her cat. And she has been angry ever since, refusing even to speak to Vera."

"But of course it's difficult to imagine Rena deliberately harming someone, even Vera," I said.

"Difficult yes, impossible no," Mrs. K replied. "And I think we must include Hannah Bissela. She and Rena are very close, and you remember how upset she was at what Vera had done to her friend, making sure that absolutely everyone knew about it."

I agreed. "And what about that poor fellow, what was his name, William something. The one who was waiting on Vera in the dining room when he accidentally spilled a little soup on her dress?"

"Yes, I remember. I think his last name was Johanson. No, Johnson. What a hoo-hah she caused. Called him such terrible names and he had to stand there and apologize and she just kept shouting at him. I never saw him serving after that day."

"No, I believe they gave him another job working outside, because I've seen him sweeping the walkways and raking leaves, about which he never looks at all happy."

I added William Johnson to the list. And doing so reminded me about another William, or Williams, the poor fellow who left the wastebasket in the wrong place in Vera's room. Mrs. K agreed he should definitely be on the list.

Before we could continue, our waiter returned with a smile on his face.

"Okay, ladies, I think I've got it now. All we have is plain and Earl Grey tea and peppermint herbal tea. And we don't have any bagels. Just toast. But that's about the same thing, right?"

Oy, the same thing? But what could we do?

"I'll have the peppermint," Mrs. K said. "And do you have a bran muffin?"

I was afraid he was going to run off again to check, but this time he smiled and said, "That I know. Yes, we have bran muffins. Would you like one?"

"Yes, please." He then turned to look at me, his pencil poised over his pad.

"The same, please," I said. Why complicate things?

As the waiter walked away, I looked around the restaurant, which now was becoming more crowded. I noticed something.

"Rose, do you see anything…anything different about the people in here?"

Mrs. K looked up from the menu, which she had been studying, and swept the room with her eyes.

"No, not really…well, yes, now that you mention it, Ida. I…"

But before she could finish what she was saying, a tall young man in a rumpled gray suit interrupted.

establishment, that is, one catering especially to gay couples, doesn't matter to you."

"Matter?" Mrs. K said. "Why should it matter? Oh, you mean we might be mistaken for being…for having a 'relationship,' as you put it? Well, yes, but that is more amusing than anything else. I mean, at our age…"

"Yes, that's my point," Andrews said. "My mistake illustrates a couple of things, such as how we tend to take things for granted that we shouldn't, and how we don't have to think of ourselves as belonging to one group or another just to eat in a good restaurant."

"Listen," Mrs. K said, "I'm sure the bran muffins here are as good as anywhere else. Maybe better, although so far I have not had a chance to find out. If the other people here don't mind that Ida and I are not hugging and *potching* each other on the *tuchis*, I'm sure we don't care if they are." I nodded in agreement.

Mr. Andrews laughed at this and said, "So I take it you don't mind my telling this little story?"

"Of course we don't, do we, Ida?"

I shook my head. "It's not every day we get into the newspaper."

Mr. Andrews shook our hands and thanked us and again walked away. And this time he didn't return, so we could finish our tea before it became cold.

"Isn't it interesting, Ida," Mrs. K said as she put down her tea cup. "For all I know, we are the only Jewish people in here. And I can see we are the only people our age. In some people's minds, with their prejudices, that makes us somehow different. In this restaurant, apparently it is only our not having a 'relationship' that makes us different. And yet really we are all the same, all just people, are we not?"

I nodded. I hadn't thought of it that way, but of course she was right. It's a funny world.

The waiter came over and brought more hot water for our tea, and when he had gone Mrs. K said, "So, Ida, finally perhaps we can get down to the business we came here for. Let's make that list we promised to Inspector Corcoran."

I again took out my notebook.

"So far we have on the list Rena Shapiro, Hannah Bissela, George Williams, and this William Johnson, or whatever his name is," I said. "Who else should we put down?"

We both were silent while we thought about this. Mrs. K spoke up first.

"What about Angela Reiskof?" she said. "Do you remember the arguments she and Vera used to have?"

How could I forget? Angela is a very political person. She takes extremely seriously what she believes in, such as the environment—she is always telling us about how we should be worrying about "global warming," for example, not that we don't have enough to worry about already—and other what you would call "liberal" positions. Many of us share Angela's views; we just don't express them with so much force. We listen to Angela and nod our heads, or shake them if we disagree, maybe offer our own two cents' worth, and let it go at that.

Vera, on the other hand, generally disagreed with Angela, and she was just as loud in saying so. Actually, I don't think Vera really believed or even cared about half the things she said; she seemed to treat Angela's little outbursts as some kind of game, in which whatever Angela said, Vera would take the opposite position and try to beat her down with it. The rest of us would usually just go as far away as we could when the two of them got into it, because it could be most unpleasant. It was like a mean person teasing a dog with a bone, the way Vera got Angela more and more angry. It seemed to amuse her. I'm not sure which one of them won most of those arguments—like I say, the rest of us usually didn't stay around to watch or listen—but I know that just mentioning Vera's name around Angela would send her temperature several degrees up. Yes, Angela definitely belonged on the list.

We both paused to think, and when I heard nothing from Mrs. K and I myself had no other ideas, I assumed we were ready to leave. But just as I was picking up the last crumbs of my muffin—it was actually quite good, if a *bissel* sweet for my taste—Mrs. K said, "What about Margaret Freid?"

"Who?"

"Margaret Freid. You remember the kerfuffle. It was just after Vera moved to the Home."

"Now that you mention it, didn't Margaret accuse Vera of some kind of hanky-panky with her husband, Ben?"

"That's right. Vera and Ben both denied it, of course, but *oy*, what a stink it caused between Margaret and Ben. And then when Ben passed last year, Margaret said it was because of all the aggravation Vera caused. I remember when her son was here for the funeral, he had some pretty harsh words for Vera. Something like it should have been her that died instead of Ben, right?"

"Yes, and I suppose that gives both of them a motive," I said, "but Margaret moved away right after Ben's death, to be closer to her children. I doubt she or her son came back here just to get even with Vera."

"I suppose you're right," Mrs. K said. "But let's put her on the list just to be complete."

And so I did.

****

When we had finished making the list, I put away the notebook and we asked for the check. After we paid, our waiter gave us a nice smile and said, "You girls have a nice day, now."

At our age, anyone who calls us "girls" must be either blind or kind. Lawrence the waiter seemed to have perfectly good eyesight, so I prefer to think he was just being nice.

Next time I shall give him a bigger tip.

Chapter Eleven

The next afternoon Mrs. K and I took a nice walk in the neighborhood after breakfast. We like to walk at least once every day, if the weather allows. Back at the Home, we found that the two policemen were waiting for us. Marilyn, the receptionist at the front desk, told us as soon as we entered the lobby.

"They said to take your time," Marilyn said. "They'll be waiting in the lounge."

Mrs. K and I went to our rooms and freshened up—to tell the truth, I got there just in time, if you know what I mean: a brisk walk at my age gets the juices flowing in more ways than one—and then I passed by her room and we went together to the lounge. Corcoran and Jenkins were sitting, reading magazines. I suppose even policemen like to take a break now and then. The only surprising thing was that while Jenkins was reading Sports Illustrated, Corcoran was holding a copy of Hadassah Magazine and seemed quite interested in the article he was reading. Both of them put the magazines down when we approached. Corcoran gave us a nice smile. Jenkins nodded.

"So, did you ladies come up with any names for us?" Corcoran asked as soon as we had sat down opposite them.

"We did," Mrs. K said. "Now, these are just people who seem to us to have had a stronger dislike for Vera

Gold than most other residents. No one really liked her, except of course her family."

Corcoran glanced at the page I handed to him. "Hmm. Not a lot to go on, but that's okay. We're just beginning our investigation." He asked Jenkins for his notes and looked them over.

"I don't see anyone on your list who has turned up in our interviews, except perhaps this Rena Shapiro, the lady with the cat? Seems like everyone remembers that incident."

He looked again over the notes, then looked up. "There are a few others who at least were or could have been in the room at some time that day. I'm told that at lunchtime, someone on the nursing staff always brought Mrs. Gold a pill to take with her lunch. We haven't been able to establish whether that actually happened on the day in question. Apparently they weren't serving meals that day, at least not on their regular schedule. I understand it was a religious holiday, wasn't it?"

"Yes, *Yom Kippur*, the Day of Atonement," Mrs. K said.

"Right. Of course. I actually knew that. So there possibly was that person. Also, in the afternoon somewhere between three and four, a member of the cleaning staff looked in to see if everything was all right, and apparently it was." He checked his notes again. "The nursing staff checked up on her several times during the day, but they didn't necessarily enter the room. I'm told Mrs. Gold did not need assistance to use the toilet and she could adjust her bed automatically." Another glance at the notes. "One curious thing was that one of the nurses said that, when she looked in on Mrs. Gold, she noticed a little pill cup on the table next to the bed, and she thought she saw one pill in it. She didn't think anything of it, as she was not assigned to help with Mrs. Gold's medicines, and since Mrs. Gold was asleep, she just closed the door and went on her way."

"And was that pill found by the bed when Mrs. Gold was later...later found deceased?" Mrs. K asked.

"Well, no. But we don't know whether that has any significance, as we don't know what kind of pill it was—if indeed there was such a pill—or whether Mrs. Gold woke up and took it. We did ask her son about it, but he said he didn't notice any pills by her bed."

More consulting the notes.

"Oh, yes. One of the serving staff whom we interviewed said she saw someone—one of the residents, she assumed, a woman—going into Mrs. Gold's room with what looked like a glass of water sometime late in the afternoon, sometime after four o'clock."

"And she knows who this woman is?" Mrs. K asked.

"Unfortunately, no. She had just started work here the day before and didn't know any of the residents by sight. Of course, we asked if she might be able to identify the person if we showed her pictures of all the women residents, but she said she only saw the back of the woman as she entered Mrs. Gold's room and wouldn't know what her face looked like. The best she could say was that she was an older woman, slender, wearing a gray dress."

"Hmm. Too bad she couldn't see the face."

"Yes, and I was hoping you ladies might be able to help. Perhaps you can somehow find out who this person was. I'm sure people here will tell you things they might hesitate to tell us. Anyway, please keep your ears open for any information about that."

This was, of course, most interesting news. What would a resident have been doing in Vera's room at that time, especially when everyone was supposedly at *Yom Kippur* services? We would just have to wait and find out.

Corcoran continued reading from his list. "Another person who has been mentioned to us is a man of about, well, let's say older than fifty, described as heavyset, even overweight, who was seen lurking in the area of Mrs. Gold's room about five p.m. We don't know who he is or whether he tried to enter the room, just that he was nearby."

Neither Mrs. K nor I could shed any light on who this might have been. But whoever he was, he was now a suspect on Corcoran's list, and therefore had to be added to our list.

As Corcoran was about to say something else, a server came by with a tray of cookies, followed by another pushing a tea cart. This was the regular afternoon snack, always a different baked goodie with tea. It is something we look forward to, not just because it's usually quite delicious, but also as a break in the afternoon routine. Sometimes it's even hard to stay awake in the late afternoon, and a little *nosh* helps to keep us from dozing off.

We all took a cookie or two from the tray and a cup of tea. And a napkin for our laps, of course, we shouldn't make crumbs on the carpet. As we were beginning to munch on the crispy cookies, Inspector Corcoran's eyes seemed to light up as if he were having a revelation of some kind. He looked at Mrs. K and said, "Do you know what kind of cookies these are, Mrs. Kaplan?"

Mrs. K said, "I believe they are ordinary

mandelbrot," she said. "It just means almond bread. Every Jewish mother bakes them. And we have a very fine baker here at the Home."

"Well, they're delicious," Corcoran said, "but more than that, they remind me of cookies I haven't had since I was a kid. You know, my grandmother on my dad's side was Jewish, and she used to bake cookies just like this for us kids. It's like being back in her kitchen."

Okay, so Inspector Corcoran making a fuss over cookies he remembers was a *bissel* surprising, especially finding out his grandmother was Jewish. (If it had been his grandmother on his mother's side, it would have made him Jewish also, because being Jewish passes from the mother to her children, but not from the father. It has never seemed fair to me, but who am I to argue with tradition?) But what was really a shock was the reaction of Corcoran's partner Jenkins.

I'm quite certain that in all the time Mrs. K and I have been in the presence of the policeman Jenkins, he hasn't once smiled or even looked like he was thinking of smiling. A real sourpuss, that Jenkins.

But as soon as he tasted the *mandelbrot*, his eyes too seemed to light up, and you would have thought he was listening to a choir of angels. In fact, he too was remembering something. Like a regular human being, he looked up and was actually smiling! And he talked like a *mensch* also.

"My grandmother wasn't Jewish," he said. "She was Italian. But these cookies taste exactly like the biscotti she used to bake. Haven't had them in years!"

"*Es gezunterhayt,* eat in good health," exclaimed Mrs. K. Anything that can put a smile on the *ponem* of sourpuss Jenkins is to be encouraged.

We all sat there *fressing* the *mandelbrot* and sipping our tea for a few more minutes, until Corcoran finally put down his cup, neatly folded up his napkin, and said, "Thanks very much for the tea and—what did you call them, *mandel*..."

"*Mandelbrot*," Mrs. K said.

"Yes, thank you. Maybe you can get me the recipe and my wife can make them. But I suppose we'd better get back on track here. I wanted to ask you whether the name Julio Melendez rings a bell."

Mrs. K looked at me and I at her, but we both shook our heads.

"Is it maybe that singer who plays the guitar?" I asked. I'm sure his name is something like that.

Corcoran laughed. "No, nothing like that. Mr. Melendez is, or at least was, one of the cleaning staff here."

"And why do you ask if we know this Mr. Mendez"? Mrs. K asked.

"It's Melendez. Well, I trust I can tell you two and it won't go any further." He glanced around us, perhaps looking for whether Mrs. Bissela was hiding under one of the cushions. The way she seems to know everything that happens here, I wouldn't be surprised. "Anyway, maybe you can find out something more about it than we have so far."

We nodded.

"Mr. Melendez, as I said, was a member of the cleaning staff. Just came on a few weeks ago. The day after he was hired, he was assigned to vacuum the hallways. He apparently was cleaning just outside Mrs. Gold's room when she came out and almost ran into Mr. Melendez. According to someone who witnessed the incident, Mrs. Gold said something sharply to Mr. Melendez. He responded, after which she shouted a racial epithet, which I won't repeat here, loud enough for the witness and anyone else in the area to hear."

Oy, again Vera is making herself popular with the staff.

"This is something I hadn't heard about. So what happened then?" Mrs. K asked.

"Apparently at this point, Melendez threw down the vacuum cleaner hose he was holding and walked away, he says to avoid saying something he would later regret, because he was so upset. Insists all he said was she should watch out. Anyway, he told his superior what had happened, and they told your Mr. Pupik."

"And Vera?"

When Pupik asked Mrs. Gold about it, she claimed he had insulted her first. Made quite a stink about it, according to Pupik."

I can imagine. And also I can imagine Pupik's reaction. He would do anything to shut Vera up once she starts on him.

"So what did Pupik do?" Mrs. K asked.

"Had the man removed from the vacuum detail, apparently, and docked him a week's pay. Poor guy quit the next week."

Mrs. K thought for a moment about this. Then she said, "You apparently have interviewed this Mendez...Melendez, whatever. Tell me, is he what you would call a heavy gentleman?"

"As a matter of fact, he is," Corcoran said, smiling. "And we are taking that into account."

Had we known all of this, Mr. Melendez would surely have been on our list. I added him now.

****

After the policemen had left, Mrs. K and I sat for a while going over what they had said (well, what Corcoran had said, as Jenkins is mostly the silent type).

As we were about to leave, Mrs. Bissela approached us, smiling and clearly with something on her mind.

"Rose, Ida. I saw you were busy talking with those two policemen. The ones who are investigating Vera's death. What did they say?"

It's not like Hannah Bissela to come right out and ask for information; usually she is getting it more indirectly. She must have been extremely anxious to find out what the policemen told us.

"Now, Hannah," Mrs. K said gently, "you know anything they told us would be confidential and not to be passed along to others." She didn't add, "At least anything you would find interesting," but I'm sure that was understood.

"Yes, but certainly there is something you can tell me."

"Well," Mrs. K said, "Inspector Corcoran did say there were some people seen in the area of Vera's room during the day she died, but they don't know who they were. A woman resident, and a heavyset man. Do you have any idea who they might be, or who might have gone into Vera's room that afternoon?"

Mrs. Bissela thought about it, then shook her head. "No, I was at the services most of the day, as you were."

Mrs. K nodded. "Well, Ida and I are making a list of whoever might have had a reason to harm Vera. We have the most obvious people...."

"Like Rena?" Mrs. Bissela said. "And Angela?"

"Yes, they certainly are the obvious ones. To be

honest, I even have you on the list, because it is well known you didn't like Vera."

"An understatement, I'm sure. By all means, include me on your list. It is quite appropriate. But of course I didn't do it. Whatever it was that was done."

"I'm sure you didn't, Hannah. And maybe you can help us with who else we should put down. You usually know more about these things than we do...."

Mrs. Bissela brightened. This was her specialty. "You have heard about the cousin, I assume? Erik Weiss?"

"The one in Singapore?" I asked.

Mrs. Bissela laughed at this. "No, no. Not Singapore. Sing Sing. It is a prison in New York."

"Prison?" Mrs. K said. "For what is he in prison?"

"I think it's for embezzlement, or something like that. He was taking money from a business he worked for, somewhere in this state, I think. Just a *ganif*, a thief. Not a nice person. I once saw a picture of him—it's a while ago, Vera showed me a photograph of the family for some reason—and he is indeed *zaftig*, quite a large man, like the person you mentioned. If not that he was in jail, I certainly would be adding him to your list, near the top."

"Why is that?" I asked. "Did he also commit a murder or...what?"

"It isn't why he's in jail, but how he got there. What I heard is that Vera, as they say in those old gangster movies, blew the whistle on him. Sold him down the river. You know, turned him in to the authorities. And testified against him."

"What do you mean? Was Vera really such a *shtunk* as to turn against her own family?"

"Well, it apparently was not as bad as that, although the cousin might not agree." Mrs. Bissela lowered her voice a bit. "What I heard is that Vera was working for the company that Erik was stealing from. He was their accountant or something. She had actually gotten him the job, had vouched for him. When she found out what he was doing—I don't know how—she told him he should turn himself in, return the money, and take his punishment. At that time I guess he hadn't taken much money and probably would not have been treated harshly. But he refused, and in fact he continued to steal the money, probably assuming Vera would never turn him in, being a close relative. If that is so, then Vera was in a real pickle, whether to look the other way and let Erik continue to embezzle from her company, or to tell them what he was doing."

"And she did tell them?"

"Yes, and then testified against him in court. And I cannot myself say I blame her. As you know, I didn't like Vera and was upset by many of the unfriendly things she did. But that isn't one of them, as far as I'm concerned. It was, as they say, a 'no win' situation."

"Yes, I agree," Mrs. K said. "But as you point out, her cousin Erik probably would not."

In a way, Vera telling on her cousin was like her telling Pupik about Rena Shapiro's cat; it was *lashon hara*. And although some might say that neither was right, I think if Vera's only purpose in speaking of Erik's crime was to prevent harm to her company, she should be excused. Nevertheless, is it a wonder that *lashon hara* is considered the most difficult sin not to commit, or that of the forty-three sins for which we ask God's forgiveness on *Yom Kippur*, eleven are committed by speaking? Vera telling on Erik, someone telling Mrs. Bissela that she had done so, and then Mrs. Bissela telling us, all technically were *lashon hara*. And now I am committing it by telling you! *Oy gevalt*, it can get so complicated.

This story of the cousin was a total surprise to both of us. But unfortunately, as the man was in prison, we could not very well add him to our list.

It was too bad, I remember thinking. He would have made a most welcome addition.

Chapter Twelve

It was about a week later that the police made an arrest for Vera's murder.

I was chatting with Mrs. K in her apartment when she received a telephone call. She said "Hello" and then just listened for a minute or so, while her face got so pale I was afraid she would faint. She sat down on a nearby chair. Finally she said, "Don't worry, dear. I'll see what I can do."

After she hung up, she just sat there as if trying to make sense of what she had heard on the telephone. I have seldom seen her looking so upset, or maybe confused. I, of course, was dying to know what—and who—it was that had caused such a reaction. So I asked.

"That was Daniel," she said in a strained voice. "He's been arrested for his mother's murder."

Yes, Daniel. *Nu*, I was as surprised as you are!

Now I too was staring into space. *Gotteniu*! How was this possible? Not only was Daniel not on our list of possible suspects, but he was probably the last person we would have thought to put there.

"Did he tell you why they had arrested him? They must have some *meshugge* theory or other, but I cannot imagine what it might be."

"He didn't really say, and I'm not certain that he knows yet. He sounds completely *farmisht*, bewildered. And I don't blame him."

112

"And why did he call you? Shouldn't he be calling a lawyer or something?"

"Oh, I assume he has called one. But he said he wanted to talk to me, and could I meet with him today or tomorrow."

"So you will do that?"

"Of course. And I hope you'll come with me."

"Yes, certainly." I could hardly refuse. And I was just as curious to find out how this could have happened as was Mrs. K.

"But first," Mrs. K said, now with a firm and determined tone of voice, she having recovered a little from the shock, "I will have a talk with Inspector Corcoran. Surely he can give us some idea why Daniel, of all people, has been arrested."

Typically, she didn't waste any time getting in touch with Corcoran, and he agreed to see us at his office that afternoon.

Before that meeting, however, and in fact all during the rest of the morning and over lunch, Mrs. K and I tried to figure out how Daniel could be not only a suspect, but the person the police had decided was in fact the murderer of Vera Gold. Of his own mother. It simply didn't make sense, at least to us.

"Let's try to be objective about this," Mrs. K said as we finished our lunch. I could hardly eat and refused second helpings of everything. "Let's treat Daniel as we would any other suspect in a crime."

"That makes sense," I said. "Surely that's the way the police are treating him."

"Exactly. And when considering a suspect in a crime, we always must look for a motive and an opportunity," Mrs. K said. "I suppose because he was helping his mother with taking her medications, he did have some opportunity to give her the wrong pills. But of course so did many other people, including several employees of the Home, Rena Shapiro, and even Fannie. People were apparently in and out of her room all day, as is normal. But even if Daniel did have an opportunity to give Vera what amounted to poison, why would he do it? What would have been his motive?"

"Well, to be honest," I said, "he did tell us that he would be getting something in his mother's will. A big something yet. That could have been his motive, couldn't it?"

"Yes, of course money is always a possible motive, so I suppose Daniel had one. But we can hardly suspect that everyone who is going to inherit from a close relative will want to murder them for the money, especially when the relative is elderly and ill."

"No," I agreed. I took a sip of water, as all of this thinking was making me thirsty. But Mrs. K was in her element, and she continued right on.

"He also said there was a gift to the Home in Vera's will. Shall we then suspect Pupik or one of the staff of killing her to get it? And do we suspect this Fred person as well? No, it's all too simple, and too unlikely. There must be more to it than that."

There usually is.

****

Inspector Corcoran's office was located downtown. Mrs. K and I again got on the shopping shuttle, which Mrs. K said would take us close enough to police headquarters that we could walk the rest of the way. As I had never been to police headquarters, *Got tsu danken* (thank God), I took her word for it.

When we boarded the bus, Andy, the shuttle driver, asked us where we were going, as usual. We of course didn't say "to the police station," but gave him the name of a store nearby. All we needed was for everyone within earshot to start nudging us about why we were going there. And once Mrs. Bissela heard about it…well, you know.

So Andy dropped us off at the usual place for shopping, and we walked a few blocks to a plain-looking building that was police headquarters. From the outside it just looked like an ordinary ugly office building; only a shiny brass plaque next to the big double front doors warned you that it was full of policemen.

Mrs. K had been to Corcoran's office once or twice since we had met him during that business with the matzoh ball soup, which is why she knew where it was. I had never been there, and I didn't like the idea of going into that building, as I watched policemen and police ladies in uniform and in plainclothes passing in and out of the doors. Even though I was of course not guilty of anything, and I honestly have only respect for policemen—after all, our good friend and table companion Isaac Taubman's son Benjamin is on the police force and is a wonderful boy—it's from my childhood in the old country that I still get a shiver when I'm around those people in uniforms. But that is just my problem and a story for another day.

Inside we faced a desk at which sat two uniformed policemen. One was busy on a computer or something, and the other was writing something on a pad. As soon as we got near the desk, the writing policeman looked up and, seeing us, gave us a nice smile, and asked if he could help us. Mrs. K said we were there to see Inspector

Corcoran, and the man at the desk immediately nodded and picked up his telephone. A few seconds later he told us to go to the second floor and we would be met there.

When we arrived at the second floor, we were greeted by Corcoran's secretary—she was wearing a pretty green blouse and brown skirt, not a uniform—and shown into his office. As he also doesn't wear a policeman's uniform, I'm not at all uncomfortable around him, or even his *shlumpy* partner Jenkins for that matter.

The first thing I noticed when being shown into Corcoran's office was his first name. On his door in gold letters it said "Inspector Robert Corcoran, Homicide." In the many times I had met Corcoran, all at the Home, he was always "Corcoran" or "Inspector Corcoran," or maybe "that handsome policeman"; this was the first time I knew his first name. I doubted I would have any occasion to use it, however.

Corcoran's office was not what you would call decorated, but it did have several photographs on the walls. Some seemed to be of him with his family, which I thought was very nice. One of the pictures was of Corcoran with two smiling young boys maybe seven or eight years old, all of them wearing skis and standing in the snow. Another was just him with a beautiful young woman I assume is his wife and mother of the two boys. It is interesting how much a few photos can tell you about a person. Some of the pictures were of Corcoran shaking hands with people like the mayor and the police chief. You know, the kind that show what important people a person knows. There also was a large map of the city on one wall and two faded prints of people on horses on another. I guess it was about right for a policeman's office.

Inspector Corcoran himself greeted us at the door. Although he had said he wanted our help, it had to be difficult for him to take time out from a murder investigation, and who knows what other important police business he had, to talk with us. Nevertheless, he certainly looked and sounded like he was glad to see us.

"Please come in, Mrs. Kaplan, Mrs. Berkowitz," he said with a smile. After asking his secretary to ask Sergeant Jenkins to come to his office, he turned his attention to us. He indicated two chairs for us to sit in. "Can I get you something to drink? Some coffee? Water?"

We both said "no, thank you," although to tell the truth, I could have used a nice cup of tea just then. But I knew Mrs. K wanted to get right to the point. And the point, of course, was Daniel Gold.

****

Inspector Corcoran took the big chair behind his desk. He was in his shirtsleeves, the cuffs rolled up, his tie loosened. The desktop was not messy, but it was crowded with papers. I wondered whether any of them had a relation to Daniel's case.

Jenkins knocked on the door and came in, pulling up a chair at the corner of the desk on the same side as Corcoran. The Inspector then said to us, "I would ask what I can do for you ladies, but I assume you're here to talk about Daniel Gold. Am I correct?"

"You are," said Mrs. K. "We cannot understand how, with all the people who one might suspect of wanting to harm Vera Gold, you have decided it was her son, who we all know was so devoted to her, who would do such a terrible thing."

Corcoran appeared very serious, putting his fingertips together and looking down at his desk before looking up at us and saying, "Yes, I fully understand. And I also understand, from what we've learned, that you, Mrs. Kaplan, have a…a special relationship with Mr. Gold, almost like family. Isn't that so?"

"I suppose you could say that," Mrs. K said. "And I'm sure that's one reason I'm here. But even if he were a stranger, I would still feel he is maybe the most unlikely person to suspect. So I am hoping you can tell us something to make some sense of it. There must be a great deal that we don't know."

"Yes, yes, there is. And ordinarily I would have to answer that I can't discuss any of the details of our case with anyone except Mr. Gold himself and his attorney. But I not only trust you—and you as well, Mrs. Berkowitz—to keep anything I say confidential, but frankly I would be glad to have you thinking about the facts together with us. You know the people involved, you know the setting, and you have a…shall we say…a unique perspective and approach to these matters. So yes, I can give you some idea of why Mr. Gold has been arrested without breaching any confidences. But keep in mind that our discussion here, like when we spoke at your residence, is strictly confidential."

We nodded.

Corcoran picked up a file folder from the right side of his desk, glanced at a few of the pages, put it down, folded his hands, and told us what was a most surprising and disturbing story.

Chapter Thirteen

"First of all," Inspector Corcoran began, "you should know in a little more detail what we've learned about the medications that apparently were responsible for Mrs. Gold's death. As I think I already mentioned, her death was caused, our medical people say, by a combination of two drugs that, when combined, can cause serious, even fatal heart problems."

Here he took out some notes from the folder he had consulted earlier and glanced down at them as he continued: "You might recall that the first drug is called ziprasidone, but let's call it drug number one, to make it easier to say." He smiled and we did as well.

"Drug number one, as I've told you, is used to treat the symptoms of schizophrenia and also episodes of…" and here he read from his notes, " 'mania, which is a frenzied, abnormally excited or irritated mood in patients with bipolar disorder.'" He looked up. "Anyway, you get the idea. Drug one is in a class of medications called…" and again he read from his notes, " 'atypical antipsychotics.' It works by changing the activity of certain natural substances in the brain." He put down the notes and looked at us. "The bottom line is that this drug, which was prescribed for Mrs. Gold by Dr. Menschyk, can affect the heart's rhythm. Therefore, taking it with some other drug that also affects the heart's rhythm can cause an irregular heart beat and be life-threatening."

I was trying hard to absorb all of this medical *megillah*, and to be honest I was finding it difficult. I glanced at Mrs. K, however, and she seemed to be nodding right along with Corcoran, not seeming lost at all. That's good, because she could explain it to me later.

"Now taking drug number one," Corcoran said, "which as I say was prescribed for Mrs. Gold, was not a problem. It was the other drug that likely caused her death. That was," with a glance down at his notes, "sibutramine. I believe I told you earlier that sibutramine, which let's call drug number two, is an appetite suppressant. It was pulled off the market a few years ago, but of course there is still some floating around in people's medicine cabinets and such. It also affects the heart's rhythm, and it is exactly the kind of drug that, when combined with drug number one, can easily be fatal. In fact, there were clear warnings on the label of drug number two against using it if you're also taking drug number one or anything similar."

"And of course this number two drug was not prescribed for Mrs. Gold?" Mrs. K asked.

"Of course. So as I've already told you, the medical examiner found evidence of both drugs one and two in Mrs. Gold's system and concluded that, especially given her weakened condition at the time, that is what caused her death."

"I see," Mrs. K said. "But as you say, you already told us this, although not in such detail. So how does it relate to Daniel?"

"Yes, I'm getting to that. One of the characteristics of drug number two, I'm told, is that it does not stay active in the system very long. In other words, if one were to take drug number two, say, in the morning, and drug number one in the evening, although there might be some slight effect, it would not be very dangerous, because number two would already pretty much be out of one's bloodstream."

We again nodded.

"Now drug number one, the drug that Mrs. Gold was supposed to take, was always given her with or just after her dinner—it's supposed to be taken with food, I believe—by her son. We assume—and in fact I don't believe he denies—that Mr. Gold gave his mother drug number one that evening, as scheduled. She died shortly after."

I wished Inspector Corcoran would call him Daniel. It was hard to remember who this "Mr. Gold" was, since we almost never called him that.

"If you consider those facts for a moment," Corcoran went on, "you'll see where I'm heading. If Mr. Gold gave his mother drug number one, and if, in order for it to be fatal, drug number two had to be given her at or at least near the same time, he is the only one who was in a position to give her both that evening."

He let this sink in for a minute. Even I could follow this reasoning. It let off the hook, so to speak, all those people who entered Vera's room, for whatever reason, earlier in the day.

Corcoran began again. "Now I know, Mrs. Kaplan, you are a big fan of Sherlock Holmes, and we've talked about the need to look for both a motive and an opportunity in these cases. Daniel Gold is the only person, or at least the only person of whom we're presently aware, who had the opportunity to administer both of the fatal drugs to his mother."

"Yes, I see," said Mrs. K. "I'm not sure you're

correct about that, but let's go on to talk about motive. I assume you will tell us that Daniel's motive was that he was going to receive a large inheritance in his mother's will?"

Inspector Corcoran looked surprised. "Well, yes, in part. But how did you…?"

"Daniel already told us this. And I don't see that it's very important. Of course he would receive an inheritance as her son, especially because he has been so good to her." Mrs. K went on to mention the point we had already discussed, that you cannot suspect everyone who receives a legacy in a will of wanting to murder that person, especially if the person is already getting toward the end of her life.

"Yes, I agree," Corcoran said after Mrs. K had finished. "And if that were the only motive Mr. Gold might have had, we would at least be less certain of our position. But there is more to consider."

"Such as?"

"Well, first of all, there's the obvious fact that he's a pharmacist. He would not only be familiar with the interactions of drugs such as these, but he would have access to them, perhaps even to those no longer on the market."

"Yes, I suppose so," Mrs. K conceded, if somewhat reluctantly.

"As you know, he was very reluctant to allow an autopsy, and as I understand it he only agreed after you, uh, put pressure on him, correct?"

"Yes, but I assume you understand that he was objecting for religious reasons. That should not be held against him."

"Perhaps. It's just something to take into account.

But there's also his financial circumstances. I can't go into detail, but suffice it to say he was, and is, in need of a considerable amount of money, and very soon."

We both were silent as we took in this bad news. We certainly could not contradict it, as we had no knowledge of Daniel's finances. Inspector Corcoran waited patiently.

Finally Mrs. K said, "So this is your case for murder? Is it not all what would be called circumstantial evidence? You are just drawing conclusions from these circumstances."

"Well, no, but before I go on, I want to point out that sometimes circumstantial evidence is all we have to go on. There's not always an eyewitness, or a smoking gun. And I believe it was Thoreau who said 'Some circumstantial evidence is very strong, as when you find a trout in the milk.'"

This seemed like a strange thing for Mr. Thoreau to say, and I didn't quite understand what a fish would be doing in the milk, but Mrs. K seemed to, as she said, "Yes, I suppose so. Still, I think you're making a big mistake. I know Daniel very well, and it's simply impossible that he would do such a horrible thing, not for all the money in the world." She was getting quite emotional.

Corcoran smiled and held his hand out as if to stop her becoming too upset.

"Mrs. Kaplan," he said, "I can well understand your feelings, and I realize you are much closer to Mr. Gold and know him better than any of us here. And I also realize that, no matter how strong circumstantial evidence is, even if that trout is definitely in the milk, it is not as conclusive as an eyewitness might be. And even eyewitnesses can be mistaken, as has been shown many times. But there is also one other piece of evidence that I must mention that may change your thinking somewhat."

"And that is?"

"Given all of these circumstances that I've already mentioned, we obtained a search warrant for Mr. Gold's home."

"A search warrant?" Mrs. K said, surprised. As was I. "For what could you be searching? The murder weapon?" Although this was a sarcastic question by Mrs. K, it turned out to have a serious answer.

"In a way, yes," Corcoran said. "Believe it or not, it's not uncommon for a criminal to fail to dispose of all evidence of his crime, either because he's so confident he won't be apprehended he doesn't need to, or just because he's careless. We were hoping to find some trace of sibutramine somewhere in his home. It was a long shot, you might say. But it paid off, because we actually found an unmarked bottle in his medicine cabinet that, when analyzed, contained a few sibutramine pills. That was when we decided to make the arrest."

At hearing this, both Mrs. K and I were, you could say, totally *tsemisht*. Confused. Even flabbergasted. Had a "smoking gun" really been found in Daniel's hand? For Mrs. K especially this was a difficult thing to accept. Could Daniel really have done such a terrible thing?

Inspector Corcoran could see how this last thing he said had affected Mrs. K and me, and he hurriedly tried to reassure us.

"I know this is very difficult for you both," he said, "and I'm sure you will continue to believe in Mr. Gold's innocence, as is quite natural. But I assure you we're quite comfortable with our judgment that Mr. Gold is indeed the guilty party here. In other words, while I'm very grateful for the help you've given us—and me in particular—to this point, now that, with your help, we've discovered the perpetrator of this crime, I'm asking you to accept our judgment and to let the process of justice run its proper course." Jenkins nodded enthusiastically at this.

Mrs. K did not look at all ready to accept Corcoran's judgment. "You are asking us to, what do they say, to butt out?" she asked. "To assume you are right in arresting Daniel?"

"Well, yes, although I wouldn't put it quite that way."

"Put, shmut, it's all the same." She stood up and turned to me.

"Come, Ida. It seems the police think this case is now closed. We have no further business here."

"Now, Mrs. Kaplan," Corcoran said, also standing, "please don't take what I said the wrong way. I really am grateful for your help, for both of your assistance. But there comes a point when no further assistance is...is required, that's all."

Mrs. K's tone softened a little. She said, "I know, Inspector Corcoran. You have to do your job the way you think best, not how I think you should do it.

"And we have to do the same."

We started to leave the office, but then Mrs. K seemed to think of something and turned back to the policemen.

"Isn't it too bad that the cousin is in jail?" she said. "He would make such a better suspect than Daniel."

Corcoran looked puzzled. "The cousin? Whose

cousin are you referring to?"

"Vera's cousin, Erik. The one who is in prison."

He still looked puzzled. "Yes, in our general background investigation we discovered the cousin, but why do you consider him important? I admit we didn't follow up with him, because he wouldn't figure in the will, or in any other way we could see."

"Well, no, he would not, because he's in prison." And Mrs. K told Corcoran what Mrs. Bissela had told us about Vera's telling on Erik.

"Hmm. As I said, we didn't really check up on him, but now that you tell me this, I think we'd better. Just to tie up loose ends, you understand. You say he's in Sing Sing prison? I'll have our records department check on that, just to make sure."

"Oh, and one other thing," Mrs. K said. "Daniel told us that a large part of his mother's estate was to go to a man named Fred Herring. No, Herrington, I think. Is he still in the will, or does everything go to Daniel?"

Corcoran hesitated before answering, but then said, "Again, I'm sure Mr. Gold will tell you anyway, and a deceased's will is a public document, so yes, Fred Herrington is still in the will. And yes," he added, holding up a hand, "we realize that gives him a motive, and we wanted to speak with him—still do—but so far we've been unable to locate him. We'll keep trying, as will the estate. But a motive without an opportunity, as you know, is very weak evidence, and at this point I can't see him having that opportunity. Or this Cousin Erik either, for that matter. So to be honest, we won't be spending a whole lot of time and effort on either man. As I said, we're quite comfortable with our present conclusions." He smiled as he said this, and Mrs. K accepted the point. *Nu*, she should argue with the policeman?

Again we turned to leave, and as we did Corcoran said, "I should remind you again that our little discussion here was in strict confidence, and I'd appreciate if you didn't discuss any of the details of this case with others."

"But it is already well known at the Home that Vera Gold was…did not die of natural causes," I said. "We cannot pretend otherwise."

"No, I don't mean that. I mean the details, like what the medications were, the timing, that sort of thing. Our investigation is continuing even though we believe we have the right person, and the less those details are spread around, the better, if you understand what I mean."

We understood, and we promised to be careful what we said. He again thanked us for coming—and no doubt was thankful also we were leaving—and we left his office.

****

On our way to the elevator, Mrs. K sat down on an upholstered bench, and I sat next to her. She looked quite pale and just sat quietly without saying anything, and I didn't disturb her. Finally she turned to me and said, with the conviction of a person who knows she is right and is prepared to fight to prove it, "Ida, we have a lot of work to do."

"But the policemen made it clear they didn't want any more help from us. It's just like in some of the cases of Sherlock Holmes, and of course you know that even better than I, where the policemen tell Mr. Holmes to, how did you put it, to butt out. To be honest, I always wondered why the policemen would not be glad to have someone of Mr. Holmes's great ability on their side. Jealousy, I suppose."

"Yes, I suppose," Mrs. K said. "But whatever the reason, I don't intend to do any such thing, any more than Mr. Holmes would. Especially as we are responsible for Daniel being in such trouble in the first place."

"You mean because we convinced Daniel to allow the autopsy?"

"Yes, because otherwise, despite Fannie's suspicions, I doubt Vera's death would ever have been called a murder."

I thought about this for a moment. "But on the other hand," I said, "it turns out it was a murder, and if there had been no autopsy, the murderer, whoever he is, would have gotten away with it."

Mrs. K sighed. "Yes, I suppose so. But as they say, it's better ten guilty men go free than one innocent man be condemned."

"And what if the policemen are right, and it really was Daniel?" I hated to say this, but *nu*, it was hardly impossible, whatever we might want to believe.

"Then we will have at least done everything possible to be sure there is no stone that was not turned over.

"Yes, we must work even harder to win Daniel's release."

I nodded in agreement, but secretly I was not so much worrying about our winning, but that we were playing for the right team.

Chapter Fourteen

Inspector Corcoran had told us that Daniel was free on bail, and we learned that, until this terrible mess was straightened out, he was what I think they called "on leave" from his job. So we gave him a call and asked if we could stop by his house on our way back.

It was a different Daniel we saw this time. He looked, as we say in Yiddish, *farmisht* and *farmatert*, confused and tired, and who can blame him? Being charged with murder will certainly put a damper on anyone's spirits.

"This is a terrible thing," Mrs. K said when we had all sat down in Daniel's living room, "that you have been arrested. Of course, the police have made a big mistake."

Daniel put his head in his hands, then looked up at Mrs. K and said, "I don't understand. Why would anyone think I would want to harm my mother, much less kill her?" His eyes were red like he had not slept.

Mrs. K put her hand on Daniel's and said, "They don't know you. They only know a few facts that they think point in your direction."

"Yes, my lawyer told me. And it's true that I'm in her will, as I already told you, and that I owe some money. But that hardly…"

He stopped talking and again put his head in his hands. When he looked up, he said, "Rose, could you help me? I know you've dealt with the police before and know something about how they work. I mean, I have a lawyer, and I'm sure he knows all the legal stuff, but he probably thinks I'm guilty and is just going to try to get me a lighter sentence or something. He won't…he won't 'investigate' for me, if you know what I mean."

Mrs. K again patted Daniel's hand. "Of course, Ida and I will do what we can."

Which of course meant we had agreed first to help Fannie find how her sister died, and now to help the person the police say killed her. *Oy*, was it getting complicated.

"We have already been to see Inspector Corcoran," Mrs. K continued. "He's a fair-minded man, and I'm sure if we can show him that he has made a mistake, he will want to correct it."

Daniel nodded his head a few times but said nothing. In fact, we all just sat there quietly for a minute, until Mrs. K said, "So, Daniel, do you have any idea at all who might have done this? As I'm sure you know, the police are convinced it had to be someone who gave your mother this bad medicine late in the afternoon or in the evening. That's why they are so sure it was you, of course. Can you think of anyone else who was in your mother's room about that time?"

Daniel scratched his head. "No, I really can't think of anyone, not while I was there. But of course I arrived a bit late because services didn't end until sundown."

"That's right," Mrs. K said. "Everything was on a different schedule on *Yom Kippur*, wasn't it? Yes, we'll have to consider that as well. Then is there anyone who you know to have threatened your mother or in any way indicated they would like to harm her?"

He shook his head. "I know she wasn't very popular

there. She could be a real bitch at times, especially to people she didn't particularly like. But want to kill her? I can't imagine it."

"No, of course not," Mrs. K said. "Well, you can be sure we will do what we can to learn the truth. Meanwhile you must try to keep up your spirits. And get some sleep. You look like you were up all night."

Daniel rubbed his eyes. "I was, or practically all night. I probably got an hour or two of sleep. And of course it's been devastating to my wife as well, as you can imagine." Daniel's wife I have not met, but there's no doubt it's an awful thing for one's husband to be accused of murder.

We stood up to leave. Daniel stood too and said, "It's such a nightmare. I mean, to be charged with murder, and of my mother…" He seemed on the verge of breaking down, but then he regained his composure and said with a try at a smile, "I really appreciate your offering to help. Please let me know if you learn anything useful. Anything at all."

"We will," Mrs. K said. She gave Daniel a hug, and I did also, and we left him looking perhaps a *bissel* more hopeful than when we arrived.

Now all we needed was to find out something to make us more hopeful as well.

Chapter Fifteen

When we returned to the Home, my niece Sara was waiting for us in the lobby. A *shayna maidel* is Sara, such a pretty girl. She doesn't usually visit without calling first, so I immediately assumed she had done so and I'd forgotten. At my age, it's the most likely thing.

"I'm sorry, Sara," I said when I saw her. "Did you tell me you would be coming to visit? It's so hard to remember anything these days...."

"No, no, I didn't call or anything, Auntie Ida. I wasn't expecting to be here, but something came up."

"Came up? Is something wrong?"

"No, nothing like that." Just then she noticed Mrs. K standing behind me and said, "I'm sorry, Mrs. Kaplan...Rose...I didn't mean to ignore you. How are you?"

"I'm fine, Sara. It's good to see you. Please don't mind me. Go right ahead with what you were telling Ida."

Sara smiled and turned back to me. "You remember my friend Flo, I assume?"

"You mean the *ganif*? The burglar lady? How could I forget?" Perhaps you remember too, the lady who helped us out when Mrs. K's matzoh ball soup came under suspicion. Anyway, it's a long story, but this Florence is really a very nice lady, even if she has this little character flaw of being a burglar.

"Well, she was telling me this morning that she just got a new smartphone.…"

"A smart what?"

"Phone. Telephone. You know…oh, maybe you don't. A smartphone is just a cell phone that does a lot of other things, like take pictures, make recordings, connect to the internet, stuff like that."

"Okay, I understand. I've heard of this. My son Morty has one. So your friend Florence has this smarty telephone. And?"

"Well, she said she was replacing her older model— it's hardly a year old, but she always likes to have the latest high-tech gadgets—and would I like it, as she wasn't trading it in. I told her I was satisfied with the one I had. But then it occurred to me that you might like to have it."

"I? What do I need such a thing for? I have a perfectly good telephone in my room."

She laughed. "Yes, I'm sure you do. But this is one you can carry in your pocket or purse, so you're always connected, and…"

"Connected? To what should I be connected?"

"No, I mean you can make or take calls wherever you are. And send messages and take pictures. Let's say you're shopping by yourself and you see something that you think Rose here is looking for, but you aren't sure. You can just pull out your cellphone and call her and ask. You can even take a picture of it and send it to her."

I thought about this for a minute. I didn't see that it was such a big deal—Mrs. K and I usually shop together anyway.

"You can also send your friends text messages or email with it. And with the camera you can do stuff like…like take selfies to share with your friends."

"Take what-ies?"

"Pictures of yourself doing stuff, or with friends, or whatever. That's why they're called selfies."

"Look, Sara, I am appreciating your thinking of me, really I am, but I need pictures of myself and telephones that are smart like a *loch in kop*, a hole in the head. You should find someone else who…"

But Mrs. K then stepped in. "You know, Ida, maybe you should consider what Sara is saying. At our age we might be a little late to join the party, but it might be worth our at least taking a look at the decorations. To be honest, I was thinking of getting one of those telephones myself sometime, although they're expensive and I'll wait awhile yet. But if Sara is offering you this one for free…"

"That's right," Sara said. "And not only that, I want to pay for your provider for the first year, as a little present, so it won't cost you anything at all."

"*Nu*, what or who is a provider?" I asked. All these new words. "And what are they providing for me?"

"That's just the company that provides the cell service. You know, like the telephone company in the old days, the one we called Ma Bell, only now there are lots of different telephone companies. You might say Ma Bell had grandkids and they've all started families of their own."

Well, as you can imagine, at this point I am getting tired of arguing, especially since Mrs. K seemed to be on Sara's side, so I just said, "Enough. You have convinced me. I accept the telephone.

"But if it turns out to be smarter than I am, I am giving it back."

****

Sara explained a few things about the phone, which was actually very cute and had a screen just like a little television set. Apparently it was actually more like a little computer, and about computers I know a little, as we have classes at the Home teaching us how to use them to send messages to our families. I thanked her and asked her to also thank her friend Florence. But then something occurred to Mrs. K.

"Uh, Sara, dear," she said, sounding almost apologetic, "your friend Florence didn't happen to…I mean, where she got this telephone…"

Sara laughed. "You mean was it stolen? No, of course not. In fact, I was with her when she bought it. Do you think I'd give my aunt hot merchandise?"

"Well, I only thought…"

"That's okay. It was a reasonable question. No, in this case, no need to worry."

I thanked her again and she went on her way.

"*Gezunterhait*!" Mrs. K said as soon as Sara had left the building. "You should use it in good health. I'm quite jealous, you know. You are now one of the very few here at the Home with a smartphone."

"Well, please feel free to use it whenever you like," I said. "I'm pretty sure I won't have much use for it. But it was very nice of Sara to think of me, and I shall make an effort to learn how it works."

"I assume Mr. Perry, who teaches us the computers, will be able to give you some help with it," Mrs. K said.

"Yes, I'll ask him. Meanwhile, I hope it doesn't start to ring, because I have no idea how to answer it."

Fortunately, it sat there quietly in my hand, and I put it away in the pocket of my dress in case it should at some later time come in handy.

And at some later time, it did.

****

Before we returned to our rooms, the receptionist handed Mrs. K a note. We sat down so she could read it better. After reading it, she looked up and there was a funny expression on her face, and I don't mean tell-a-joke funny.

"Ida, this is a note from Inspector Corcoran. It didn't take him long to find out about Erik Weiss. Vera did help put him in prison, and he was indeed in Sing Sing."

"What do you mean, 'was'?"

"He was released two months ago. And one other thing Corcoran learned."

"And that is…"

"Erik Weiss is definitely overweight."

We added Erik to our list. In capital letters.

Chapter Sixteen

When I met Mrs. K for breakfast the next morning, something seemed different about her, and it took me a minute to figure out what it was.

"Rose, you're wearing lipstick. That seems unusual when you aren't going anywhere special. But it looks very nice."

"Thank you, Ida," she said. "I just thought I would put some on this morning. I'm surprised you noticed."

When we got to our table, Karen Friedlander and Isaac Taubman were already seated. Taubman, always the gentleman, got up and pulled out a chair for Mrs. K. He then did the same for me.

I noticed that Karen was unusually quiet. Now Karen is always a quiet one, like a little mouse, but even a mouse squeaks now and then. From Karen hardly a squeak all through breakfast, and looking so unhappy, whereas she's usually quite cheerful. I wondered whether something might be bothering her, and I asked her after breakfast if anything was wrong, but she just waved her hand and said everything was fine. It sounded like one of those uses of "fine" that really means "everything is not fine, but I don't want to talk about it."

Mrs. K had an appointment to keep after breakfast, and Karen walked away right after she told me she was fine, so that left only me and Taubman sitting and relaxing, sipping the last of our tea. (Well, he was having coffee, but it's the same idea.)

"Isaac," I said, "did you notice that something seemed to be bothering Karen? I mean she hardly said a word and was looking really depressed. It isn't like her. Have you some idea what might be bothering her?"

"No, not at all," Taubman said. "In fact, we were having a very nice discussion before you and Rose got here, and she seemed her usual self." But look who I was asking! Men never notice anything about other people unless you point it out to them.

"What were you discussing?"

"Oh, nothing much, certainly nothing to cause Karen any stress. You know, about Pupik trying to cut back on the food budget, my son's recent trip to Europe, that sort of thing." He stopped and looked thoughtful for a moment, then continued, "Oh, and I was telling her that I had asked Rose to accompany me to that new play at the Palace Theater downtown."

Oy gevalt, men can be such *shlemiels* when it comes to ladies! I mean, Isaac Taubman is a real *mensch*, always a gentleman, and very smart. He was married many years before his wife, Myra, passed away. And yet he seemed, as they say, to have not a clue what might be bothering Karen.

It was not my place to tell him. But I did need a little more information.

"You say you were having a pleasant discussion with Karen?"

"Yes, absolutely. She seemed in quite good spirits."

"And did you notice a change in these spirits at any time during your conversation?"

Taubman thought about that for a moment before answering. "Hmm. Now that you mention it, her demeanor did seem to change just at the end of our conversation, just before you and Rose showed up."

"Is that when you were telling her about asking Rose to attend the play with you?"

"Well, yes, but I don't see…"

"No, of course not. Don't worry about it, Isaac. It's nothing."

"If you say so, Ida. Perhaps Karen just had a bit of indigestion."

"Yes, perhaps. Well, I shall see you at lunch."

****

I went back to my room to rest and make a few telephone calls—using my old-fashioned telephone without the TV set in the middle. About an hour later, Mrs. K called and suggested we meet in the lounge and go over some of the information we had regarding Vera's death, so we could decide what to do next.

We walked over together and found a nice sofa in a quiet corner where we could talk without being overheard.

"Before we talk about Vera," I said when we were seated, "I wanted to ask you about something else." I fluffed up a pillow behind my back, because some of these sofas they make so deep, only one of those basketball players who look like they are standing on stilts could sit up straight without one.

"What is that?"

"First, is there some particular reason you're wearing lipstick this morning? I mean, usually you don't dress up for breakfast."

Mrs. K looked just a *bissel* embarrassed, and even might have blushed slightly, or maybe it was my imagination. But she didn't answer directly.

"Can't I decide to put on a little lipstick without it being made into a whole *megillah*? A federal case?"

"Of course. Well, maybe I should explain why I ask. Did you notice this morning at breakfast that Karen was not...was not looking very happy?"

Mrs. K thought for a moment, then said, "Yes, now that you mention it, she did look a bit *farklempt*. Upset, like she was going to cry. Why? Did you learn something was wrong? Is it something about her family? Someone close to her?"

"No, no, nothing like that, I'm pretty sure. In fact, in a way it might be just the opposite. Someone not close enough."

Mrs. K looked at me as if trying to figure out what I was talking about. I explained.

"Taubman and I were talking after you and Karen both left the table." I repeated my conversation with Taubman. "Do you now see what I'm getting at?"

Mrs. K doesn't generally have to have things spelled out for her, and this was no exception. Now she definitely did blush.

"You are suggesting," she said, "that Karen was upset because Isaac asked me to go to a play with him?"

"Doesn't that seem logical?"

"Well, perhaps. But that would mean Karen has...has her eye on Isaac, and thinks I am...what is the expression? Cutting her out?"

"It seems like it, doesn't it? Perhaps she was hoping he would ask her to accompany him to the play. Or perhaps she was planning to make her own move in his direction."

Here I should mention, if it isn't obvious, that eligible men are a relatively scarce commodity in a

140

retirement home like ours. Because we ladies tend to live longer than the gentlemen, which I am sure is all part of God's plan, once we pass the age of seventy or so there are many more of us than there are of them. That makes the ladies-to-gentlemen ratio here, where most of us are well over seventy, heavily in favor of the ladies. And several of the men who are living here are already married, like Sol Lipman. As a result, the competition for those relatively few eligible gentlemen, at least those who are most desirable because they have all their marbles and no disturbing physical or mental deficiencies, can be, shall we say, intense. Now neither I nor Mrs. K has felt the need to enter this competition, at least not in the past; but I wondered whether perhaps that had changed on her part.

Mrs. K shook her head slowly. "It's hard to believe. We've been eating at the same table for how many years? Now she decides she will get cozy with Taubman?"

"It happens. But look at it the other way. Only now does Taubman decide to ask you out. I'm sure there were reasons he didn't before, but…"

"Yes, I see. *Nu*, so how do we make Karen feel better without my telling Taubman he should take her to the play instead of me?"

"Don't be silly," I said. "I think it's wonderful you two are…are getting better acquainted. At least it's not with someone like Moishe Klein, with whom as I told you I am not interested in relating."

Mrs. K laughed. "Yes, you had given me that impression. But I think we both like Isaac Taubman and it could be very…very pleasant to go to a play with him."

"And afterward," I added, maybe raising my eyebrows just a little bit, "who knows?"

Now Mrs. K really did blush, so unusual for her. "Don't be silly, Ida. Act your age. Anyway, I shall give the matter of Karen some thought. But first we really must get back to saving Daniel from his terrible situation. That's far more important than how Karen—or I, for that matter—might feel about Isaac Taubman."

I had to agree with this. Karen would have to wait.

****

It was at this point that I suddenly got the feeling someone was watching us. You know, nothing specific, just a feeling. I looked around, thinking maybe Mrs. Bissela was snooping as she tends to do, but I didn't see anyone at all within snooping distance. My imagination playing tricks.

"You know, Ida," Mrs. K said, nicely shifting the gears, "we probably should be trying to figure out who it was who was seen to enter Vera's room in the late afternoon. If the bad medicine had to be given to her shortly before the good medicine, that pretty much lets out everyone who visited her, or gave her anything, in the morning or early afternoon."

"Yes, that does seem to narrow it down."

"Which is either a good thing or a bad thing, is it not? It narrows down the possible suspects, which is good, but it leaves us fewer alternatives to Daniel, which of course is bad."

"So are there any other suspects at all?" I asked.

"Of course there are. We just haven't identified all of them yet. So as I say, we should begin with the woman Corcoran mentioned."

"He didn't seem to have many details."

"No, all we know is that it was a woman resident. An older woman of slight build."

"And wearing a gray dress, wasn't she?"

"Yes, that's what I remember as well."

"*Nu*, this fits maybe half of the residents of the Home. How do we find the right one?"

She sighed. "Yes, we must find a way to narrow it down further."

We both sat for a few minutes, thinking. Of course, Mrs. K can do a lot more thinking in that time than I can, so I was not surprised that she was the first to speak up.

"Ida," she said, "I think there is a way we can narrow it maybe to one person."

"And how is that?"

"Remember that it was on *Yom Kippur* that Vera was killed, or at least she died right after it ended. So where was almost everyone all that day?"

"In *shul*, of course," I said. On *Yom Kippur*, if you were not aware, almost every Jew attends services at least in the morning. Even those who never attend another service all year. Most are at services the entire day. And we are supposed to fast all day as well, eat nothing from sundown to sundown, which is how Jewish holidays are counted. It's not easy for us older people to fast, it requires will power and discipline, but most of us try. At least at the Home there is a chapel right there next to the lounge, so we don't have to go anywhere else, like to a local synagogue, for services either on holidays or on Friday nights for *Shabbos* services.

"Yes, and you'll recall that we were sitting near the door, because it makes it easy to go out to the bathroom or to stretch our legs."

"Yes, I remember."

"Well, think about who was there, those we could see. Karen Friedlander and Isaac Taubman were sitting to our right, were they not?"

"Yes, I think so." I wondered whether Karen had arranged it that way. "And Fannie was at the end of our row, as was Big Wasserman." That is tall Mr. Jacob Wasserman, which is to distinguish him from short and round Abe Wasserman, whom we call "Little Wasserman." It is a little joke we have, and it also avoids confusion.

We went through a list of the other people we saw at the service and tried to remember which of them stayed until the end of the day. That would be at what is called the *Neilah* service, at which we pray for forgiveness for our sins as, we are told, "the gates of Heaven are closing." At the very end, there is sounded a long, loud note on the *shofar*, the ram's horn that has been used to announce important events and days since biblical times.

"It had to be about the time of the *Neilah* service that someone gave Vera that medicine," Mrs. K said. "And shortly after the service, Daniel arrived. So I think it's likely that anyone who was there through *Neilah* can be crossed off the list of suspects. At least for the present."

I agreed, and we tried to remember who was there when we finally stood up and stretched at the end of the service.

"Well," I said, "we certainly hugged several people and wished them *l'shanah tova*," which is like "Happy New Year." "Taubman and Fannie and…"

"Wait a minute," Mrs. K said, interrupting. "Now I remember. Sometime during the *Neilah* service, Rena Shapiro left the chapel. I remember because she passed right by us and I noticed she had a strange look on her face. I thought maybe she was not feeling well, from the fasting, you know. And yes, I'm sure she was wearing a gray dress."

I tried hard to remember the same thing, but I couldn't, and I said so. I of course took Mrs. K's word for it that Rena left the service early, but if so I didn't see it.

"What I do remember," I said, "is that Rena was not one of the persons I hugged and wished *l'shanah tova.*"

"Nor did I," Mrs. K said. "Yes, I'm certain she left early."

"And of course she's one of the people on our list of suspects," I said. "And now that I think of it, she used to be a nurse, and would know about medicines and such, so…so what do we do now?"

Mrs. K thought about that for a moment.

"I think we should first talk with Rena," she said. "Before we pass this along to Inspector Corcoran, I would like to hear what Rena has to say."

"Yes," I agreed, "maybe we're making a mistake, barking at the wrong bush, as they say."

"Tree," Mrs. K corrected. "Barking up the wrong tree. But yes, we shall have a talk with Rena."

If nothing else, I thought, considering how much Rena disliked Vera, it should be an interesting talk.

Chapter Seventeen

That evening after dinner, I asked Mrs. K what she planned to do about Sol and Lily Lipman, not to mention Lily's mother.

"You did tell Sol you would try to think of something."

"Yes, I know. And I've been thinking about it, when I haven't been thinking about Daniel, but the something has taken its time to appear. I do, however, have one little idea."

"*Nu*, what is that?"

"Well, I was thinking that it would be helpful if we could convince Lily that it would be best if her mother left. Because like I told you the other day, if we somehow found a way to force her mother out, especially if it appeared to be Sol's doing, it might leave Lily more upset with Sol than before, and blaming him for making her mother leave. So it would be better to have Lily make that decision."

"And how do we get Lily to do that? Why should she want her mother to leave, especially after Sol has been unable to convince her?"

"Well, you know of course that Lily is the kind of woman who, as my mother used to say, would go to the store for five cents worth of vinegar, and bring her own bottle."

"Yes, that's Lily, all right. A nice woman, but tight

like a fist with her money. Not at all like Sol that way."

"Exactly. And as the Yiddish saying goes, 'A miser guards his money like a dog guards its bone.'"

"Yes. But how does this help to make Lily evict her mother?"

"It's just that I recalled when Rena had that trouble with Pupik over her cat, and I checked our agreement with the Home to see if it really forbids us to have pets, I noticed that the agreement also forbids us to have more people living in our apartment than we are paying for. Wait here and I'll show you."

She got up and left the lounge, and a few minutes later she returned with some papers in her hand.

"Here is the agreement. You know, Ida, a document like this is so important, containing all the rules and regulations, what we have agreed to and what the Home has agreed to, but I'll bet not one in ten of us can remember most of what it says. We sign it and put it away somewhere safe and don't look at it again until…well, until a time like this. And I only had a vague recollection of this.…" She began to scan the papers in her hand, looking at them closely, the printing being quite small.

"Now somewhere here it says…" She looked carefully at each paragraph until she found what she was looking for. "Ah. Here it is. It says: 'Paragraph Five: Exclusive Occupancy. This agreement is for the exclusive occupancy of the Resident(s) named in Paragraph One.'" Here she turns back to the first page and says, "In Paragraph One is written my name, 'hereinafter referred to as the Resident(s).'" She flips pages forward again. "And then this Paragraph Five goes on: 'No other person than the aforementioned

Mark Reutlinger

Resident(s) is permitted to live in the Unit'—that is what they call an apartment—'without the written permission of the Management'—that is Pupik, of course. 'Should permission be granted and another person be added to the number of residents in said Unit, he or she shall be charged at the same monthly rate as the Resident, subject to the standard discount for multiple occupancy.'"

"Yes, yes," I said, "I understand. That is like Sol and Lily living together. They of course must pay for two people, not just one, but not quite twice as much. But what has that to do with Lily's mother? She is not actually living there."

"I'm getting to that. Let me find the other paragraph. Yes, here it is: "Paragraph Seven: Visitors. A visitor or visitors may stay in a Resident's Unit without charge for a maximum of two weeks in any twelve-month period. Any visitor staying in a Resident's Unit longer than said maximum shall be considered an additional Resident within the meaning of Paragraph Five and shall thereafter be charged accordingly."

Oy, so many "hereinafters" and "aforementioneds," it made my head swim. I suppose they are paying the lawyers by the word, and longer words are more expensive than shorter ones. "So please, in English, what does it mean?" I asked.

"It means that after Lily's mother was staying in their apartment more than two weeks, and I believe Sol said she has been there now for almost a month, according to the residency agreement, she must start paying rent just like everyone else."

"Yes, I see now," I said, "How clever of you to have remembered that. And of course treating Lily's mother as a resident would be quite expensive."

"Yes, and expensive for Lily and Sol, as I'm pretty sure Lily's mother is not a wealthy woman."

"So do you plan to tell Lily this? Or better yet, tell Pupik?"

"No, no. That would be almost like Vera telling him about Rena's cat. It is not my business to…to snitch on Lily. And it is also not my business to tell Lily myself."

"Well," I said, "you could tell Hannah." That is Mrs. Bissela, you will recall, the *yenta*. "It would take less than a day for it to make its way around the Home and reach Lily's ear."

Mrs. K laughed. "No, Ida, that would be worse than just telling Lily or Pupik directly. It would be like announcing it over the loudspeaker they use to tell us things like when the bus is leaving. No, it is not our job to reveal the Lipmans' little secret to the whole world."

"But if you don't tell anyone, what good is it that Lily's mother staying would be so expensive? How does that help Sol?"

"I didn't say I would not tell anyone, just I would not tell Lily or Pupik or the entire Home. I shall simply tell Sol. He is the one who asked for our help. And after all, it is his apartment and his money too that's at risk, and his mother-in-law that's the problem. It's almost my duty to alert him to this. I will merely remind him of what the agreement says. What he chooses to do with the information is up to him."

I was pretty sure I knew what Sol would do with this information.

I knew for certain what I would do with it in his place.

"Yes, I see what you're saying. But we also didn't want to put Sol in the position of being responsible for

Lily's mother leaving. It should be Lily's doing, you said."

"Oh, I'm sure it will be. I will suggest to Sol he tell Lily what he has discovered, but leave it up to her to decide whether they should pay for another tenant or send her mother home. I am quite certain what Lily will choose to do, and she won't need any urging from Sol to do it. On this I would be willing to bet."

When Mrs. K is as certain as she sounded on this, taking that bet would be most unwise.

Chapter Eighteen

It was not difficult arranging a talk with Rena Shapiro. After all, most of us at the Home do not have very busy schedules, and finding us usually means merely knocking on our door or, if we're not there, checking a few places like the lounge, the library, and the recreation room. And the restroom, of course.

It was in the library that we found Rena the next morning after breakfast. She was reading some very large book that looked like the encyclopedia, resting it on the long table that runs down the middle of the room. She looked up when we entered and nodded slightly, then went back to her reading.

Mrs. K sat down quietly next to her. I pulled out a chair and sat down across the table from them. As Rena was turning a page, Mrs. K said, "Rena, dear, when you are finished with your reading, could Ida and I have a brief talk with you?"

Rena looked up with a slightly puzzled expression and said, "A talk? That sounds a bit formal, like you don't just want to *shmooze*, but you have something on your minds. Is that right?"

"Well, actually we do. Have something on our mind, that is. And it's quite important, so when you are finished...."

Rena put a marker in the page she had been reading, took off her reading glasses, and looked at Mrs. K.

"Let us talk now. If it's important, the book can wait." She looked expectantly from Mrs. K to me and back.

Mrs. K looked around the small room. "Well, I suppose this is as good a place to talk as any. We are alone, and the room is soundproof."

Now Rena looked positively alarmed. "Soundproof? Why should soundproof matter? What do you want to talk about that needs soundproof?" Her voice was rising.

Mrs. K gestured with her hand that Rena should be quiet. "*Sha*, Rena. It's just that what we have to say is…is somewhat confidential."

"So tell me already. Is it bad news?"

"No, nothing like that. Let me explain. You of course remember that poor Vera Gold passed on *Yom Kippur*, or just after."

"Of course." Rena's tone now sounded more wary than alarmed. "We all know that. Very sad." She didn't sound like she meant that at all.

"Yes, well you probably also know that the police suspect that Vera was…was…that she met with foul play. That someone, shall we say, hurried her along to passing."

"You mean that she was murdered? I have heard the rumor, but I ignored it. Sometimes the rumors that get started around here…"

"Yes, that is so. But it happens that this rumor is true; at least the police believe it is."

"All right, so Vera Gold was murdered. A terrible thing. *Nu*, what has that to do with me?"

Now Mrs. K had decided beforehand that the best approach to Rena would be to assume it was she who entered Vera's room in the afternoon. If we were right,

Rena just might admit it. And if we were wrong about that, it would be a bit embarrassing, but no real harm done. So Mrs. K came right out and said, "It's just that you were seen going into Vera's room in the late afternoon."

You could see plainly on Rena's face the effect this statement had on her. Although she tried not to show it, it was as if someone had given her a *potch* on the *tuchis*—a slap on the behind—when she didn't expect it.

She said, "I don't know what you're talking about. I was in services all afternoon."

"Not all afternoon," Mrs. K said. "We saw you leave during *Neilah*, and you did not come back."

Rena was silent for a while, as if deciding what to say or do next. Apparently she decided that it was better to tell the truth than to try to make up a story then and there. It's difficult enough to tell a good lie, much less a lie that one hasn't rehearsed. She put one hand on her forehead and shook her head slowly from side to side. Finally she said, looking at both of us, "Yes, yes, I did go into Vera's room. I am ashamed to admit that ever since she told Pupik about my cat…well, I have let my anger build up. And I saw what other hateful things she had done to others, like that poor man who was waiting on her."

"Yes, we all seem to have suffered in some way from Vera," Mrs. K said.

"Anyway," Rena went on, "I was not sorry to hear of Vera's illness and that she might soon pass on, and I was not happy to hear that she was getting much better. Again, I am ashamed of having these feelings, they are sinful, but they would not go away."

"We all have feelings from time to time that we

would not like to admit," Mrs. K said. "It is what we do about them that matters." I nodded in agreement.

"That's just it. That afternoon, I left the service to get a drink of water. As I was passing Vera's room, I had this crazy idea that I might somehow…might somehow…as you said, hurry her along."

"Do you mean…"

Rena just nodded. I could see tears were forming in her eyes, and she took a pretty silk handkerchief from her pocket and dabbed at them.

"Hurry her along…how?" Mrs. K asked.

"Oh, I didn't have any particular plan in mind. It was just a spur-of-the-moment thing. Everyone was in *shul* and no one was around to see me—or so I thought—and so I opened the door and looked in. Vera was asleep, so I went in quietly and shut the door. I went over to her bed—I could hear her breathing—and just stared down at her for maybe a minute or two. I could so easily have smothered her with a pillow or…or anything…"

"But you didn't," Mrs. K said.

Rena looked up. "No, I didn't. I would like to think it was because whatever I might think about doing, I was too good a person to actually do such a terrible thing. And maybe I am. But I think in this case it was also a matter of…of timing."

"Timing?" I said. "I don't understand."

"I mean when this all happened. Suddenly I realized that it was not just any day, but *Yom Kippur*, the Day of Atonement. I had been spending most of the day asking God to forgive me for the sins of the past year, and promising to do better in the next year. Even assuming I was capable of such a terrible thing in the first place— *kholile*, God forbid—how could I do it on *Yom Kippur*?"

"So what did you do?" Mrs. K asked in a gentle voice.

"Do? I quietly left Vera's room and I went to my own room and lay down on the bed. All I could think of was how close I had come to doing a horrible thing. But at the same time I was very glad that I had not done it. God stopped me. I know He did."

Silence. What could one say?

Then Rena looked up, tears now rolling down her wrinkled cheeks, and said like she was pleading, "Rose, I didn't kill her, did I? I mean, you say it's true she did not die of...of natural causes, that someone killed her. Could I have done it and then not remember? Have I somehow erased it from my memory because it was such a terrible sin?" No doubt this fear had been in the back of her mind ever since Vera died.

Mrs. K took Rena's hand. "No, Rena dear," she said, "that at least is absolutely certain. What killed Vera, according to the police doctors, was...well, let's say it was something like poison. It was nothing you did or could have done. Whether it was God who stopped you or just your own good conscience, you definitely were not responsible for Vera's death."

Rena said nothing but gave Mrs. K a hug. She again took out her hanky and wiped her eyes. She even smiled now a little. Finally she spoke:

"Thank you, Rose. And you too, Ida. I'm glad I told someone about this; it has been such an awful thing to keep hidden in my mind. And I'm even happier you've assured me that I did not do what...what I almost did."

And that was all she seemed to be capable of saying.

****

"Ida, I think Rena was telling us the truth," Mrs. K

said as we closed the library door behind us. "I think it happened just the way she said: She had the evil intent and even got close to acting on it, but she couldn't carry it out. She is just not that kind of person. What do you think?"

"I agree," I said, "and I think she has suffered a lot just from having had that intention. So do we tell Inspector Corcoran what we have learned, so he doesn't pursue the mysterious woman with the glass of water any further?"

"Hmm, that's a good question. On the one hand, it would save Corcoran a lot of *tsuris* if he could cross Rena—or the person he doesn't know is Rena—off his list. But on the other hand, if we tell him it's Rena he is looking for, he may not take our word for it that she is innocent, and she will be dragged into the investigation."

"But won't he eventually figure out it's her? After all, we did."

"You're right, he will. But if we can solve this case before he does, there will be no problem."

"I suppose so. But it seems to me if we now cross Rena off our list, that leaves only Daniel as someone who could have given Vera that bad medicine, does it not?"

Mrs. K didn't answer right away. Finally she said, "No, there is also the *zaftig* man seen near Vera's room who was mentioned to us by Inspector Corcoran. Besides, even if it seemed to leave only Daniel, it only means there is someone else who could have done it, and who actually did do it, who we just haven't discovered yet. And that is what we must do very soon."

Chapter Nineteen

In the afternoon, Mrs. K and I are sitting on a sofa in the lounge, sipping our tea and reflecting on the events of that day, when I see Moses Klein heading in our direction. You remember Moishe Klein—"Motorcycle Moishe"—who I told you was suggesting I should go riding with him on his motorcycle and maybe we should get to know each other better.

I nudged Mrs. K and nodded in Moishe's direction. She patted my arm and said, "Don't worry. He's probably just looking for a place to sit. I still think he has forgotten all about inviting you to go riding with him."

That's what I thought too, since he had not mentioned it the last time we met, so I relaxed and went back to sipping my tea.

But Moishe was not just looking for any place to sit; he was looking to sit next to me! And that is what he did.

"So, Ida," he said immediately upon sitting down, "are you coming riding with me?" Apparently Moishe is one of those people who can forget something completely, and then remember it the next day.

"No, Moishe, I don't think so," I replied. "It's not something I would enjoy doing." I refrained from adding "with you," not wanting to hurt his feelings, but perhaps that was a mistake, because he was not discouraged at all by my refusal.

"But have you ever tried it?" he asked. "Have you

ever ridden on a motorcycle?"

"Well, no, but I'm sure I wouldn't like it. And it looks to be very dangerous."

"Nonsense! That's just because the newspapers like to play up stories about accidents and motorcycle gangs and things like that. I have been riding for almost my whole life, and I'm still here, aren't I?"

"Well, yes, but…"

"And if you don't try it, you'll never know if you like it, will you? Listen, we're not getting any younger, you and I, and we should be having all the new experiences we can, while we can." This last he said while leaning close to me, in a tone that suggested the kind of "new experiences" generally reserved for teenagers with out-of-control hormones.

I did my best to discourage him and continued to decline his invitation, but he continued to try to convince me. Fortunately, before I was tempted to accept just to get him to go away, Mrs. K, who had of course heard the entire conversation, spoke up.

"Ida, dear, remember you have an appointment to get your hair done in a few minutes. I think we had better be going."

Moishe looked at Mrs. K as a child might look at a parent who has said it's time to turn off the television and go to bed, but he was enough of a *mensch* not to want to interfere with my "appointment," and he simply said, "So think about it for another day or two, Ida. I'm sure you will change your mind when you think about it." As he stood up, I realized that without my noticing he had taken my hand, which he now gave a squeeze and let go. He nodded politely to Mrs. K, and left us.

For many seconds Mrs. K and I just stared at each

other. Finally she said, "I guess I was wrong, Ida. Moishe is far from giving up. In fact, he appears to be quite determined to convince you."

"And how do I convince him that he will not convince me?" I asked.

"Let me give that some thought," she said. "I'm sure there is a way, without being very rude or hurtful. He is, after all, a nice man who means well. He's just a bit *farmisht*. Just a little mixed up. But I will think of something."

****

So much confidence do I have in Mrs. K, that I didn't really worry about Moishe's *mishegoss*, or even think much about it, until the next day, when it was Mrs. K who brought it up.

"Ida, I have been talking with Little Moishe. You know, Moishe Klein's son, the one who takes him riding on his motorcycle."

"And about what have you been talking with him? About his father wanting me to go riding with him?"

"As a matter of fact, yes. I called him and explained that his father is pressuring you to ride with him, and that you don't want to, but also you don't want to hurt his feelings. And do you know what he suggested?"

"That I should just tell him no? That does not…"

"No, no. He suggests you should agree to go."

"What, is he *meshugge* like his father?"

"I don't think so. What he says is that he is aware of his father's wanting you to ride with him, because Moishe has been talking about it to him also. He thinks Moishe will not so easily get the idea out of his head, and it would be best to play along with it."

"What? And be killed? And should I also begin a

'relationship' with him? Maybe we should smooch on the sofa like two teenagers?"

"Well, actually these days teenagers do more than smooch, I'm afraid. But no, that's not it at all. He explained to me that Moishe has not actually driven his motorcycle for maybe twenty years or more, not since he was much younger and stronger. That is why Little Moishe comes and takes him out for rides. He really misses riding, but cannot manage it himself anymore."

"So why then does he invite me to ride with him?"

"It's apparently like a fantasy. He has forgotten he cannot handle the big machine, and in his mind he thinks he is still the man he was when he was fifty, or even younger. He has begun to *kvetch*, to complain that Little Moishe will not let him drive his own motorcycle, and he constantly nudges his son to let him be the one in front driving. His son says he needs perhaps a little dose of reality to bring him back to the real world."

"And I should be killed so Moishe can become real again? That is the big plan?"

"Of course not, Ida. Moishe's son assures me there is no way his father can even start that big machine, much less drive it. It is an old model, and it uses what they call a kick starter."

"What, you have to kick it?" That didn't sound very good for the machine, or your foot.

Mrs. K laughed. "No, that's just what they call it. I'm sure you have seen when the rider steps on a lever or pedal or something and pushes it down to start the engine. It's like they used to have a crank to start a car engine."

"Yes, I've seen that. I didn't know it was called kicking it. But they must just push a button now, like for a car."

"Of course. But when this motorcycle was made, it also had the kick starter. According to Little Moishe, it had an electric starter thing too, but that has not worked in years; only the kick starter works."

"And are you sure Moishe cannot work this kick starter?"

"Well, you have seen Little Moishe, how big he is. He says it takes all of his weight and quite a lot of effort to start it. And once started, it's quite heavy and he doubts his father would be able to keep it upright, or even get it off its stand. It's a machine for a strong young man, which his father once was, of course, but no longer is."

"So I should agree to go riding with Moishe, because he will be unable to start or hold up the motorcycle?"

"Yes, that's the idea."

"And what do you think of this idea? Isn't it better just to tell him no? Either way he will be disappointed. And didn't we want to avoid embarrassing him or hurting his feelings?"

"Yes, and I suppose there would be some embarrassment involved, but this way he at least will have to realize he cannot ride by himself, so he won't continue to bother either you or his son about it."

I thought about this for a moment.

"Okay, I understand what you're saying, and I suppose it will, as you say, give Moishe a 'dose of reality.' But it will be a very bitter medicine, I'm afraid."

"*Nebach*. It's a pity, yes. But after all, an *alter kocker* like Moishe—an old man of his age—should not be riding around on machines meant for much younger people, and he will just have to accept that."

Mrs. K was right, of course, so we set out to make a plan.

****

The next time Moishe approached me I was sitting by myself reading the latest issue of Time magazine and he came and sat next to me. He had a look on his face like a dog that has just spotted a juicy bone that he would like to carry off and bury. This time I was ready for him.

"Ida," he began, "here I am again to ask of you: Will you come riding with me? It is really quite safe, and…"

"Yes, I think I will."

Moishe looked as surprised as if I had just turned into a *golem*, a magical creature. This answer clearly he was not expecting.

"Eh, you will? Is that what you said?"

"Yes, that is what I said. When will this ride happen?"

"Well, mmm, I don't know. That is, I'll let you know." He looked very uncomfortable. *Nu*, there is a big difference between the asking and the doing: The one is very easy and safe; the other has many risks and complications. Mrs. K had told me this might happen, and once again she was right.

"How about tomorrow, then?" I said. "Why not get it over with?"

"Well, okay, I guess tomorrow is good. Yes, tomorrow. I shall come by at…at eleven in the morning, if that's convenient."

"Certainly," I said. "I'm looking forward to it. A new experience, as you have said." God forgive me for the lie, but it was for a good cause.

And so the next day Moishe knocked on my door at precisely eleven o'clock. I'm sure he was not expecting what he saw when I opened the door, any more than he had been expecting me to accept his offer the previous day.

I should mention that as part of her plan to put an end to the constant *nudging* by Moishe, Mrs. K had arranged with Little Moishe to borrow from his wife a black leather jacket with knobbly silver things all over it and maybe twenty-five zippers going every direction—I cannot imagine what they put in all those pockets; maybe they carry a lot of loose change—together with some black leather things that look like someone lost the back half of their trousers. They go over the legs, like what those cowboys in the old movies wore when riding their horses after the bad guys. I think they're called chaps. There was also a large black helmet, shiny black with a bright orange zig-zag stripe on the sides and a hinged part in front with a little window where you look through that could be pushed up out of the way, I assume so the person inside could sometimes see and breathe, because when it was pulled down it was like being in a very small, dark closet.

I didn't have the helmet on yet, of course. Instead I was wearing a little *shmatteh*, a little colored rag, on my head that I am told motorcycle riders wear under their helmets. If your mother came from Russia or Poland and wore a *babushka* on her head, it looked something like that, only sillier.

Anyway, Mrs. Little Moishe was obviously not my size, so when I put on her jacket and chaps—I had to borrow a pair of denim pants from Mrs. Gerbach, who wears them to work in the garden—*oy gevalt*, I looked exactly like...well, let me put it this way: I once saw a movie about a gang of young men who rode big motorcycles and wore the black leather jackets with the zippers and the black leather pants and went around making trouble for everybody. So if you looked at that movie in one of those curvy mirrors at the amusement park that makes you look like you are bulging out here and skinny there and ridiculous all over, you would have more or less what I looked like when I opened the door to Motorcycle Moishe. I know because I did look in the mirror, and even without the curvy part that is what I looked like. Mrs. K said it was the perfect outfit. For the circus, maybe. And with the helmet on, it should be maybe a space circus.

Whatever Moishe was expecting, then, it was not what he was looking at when I answered the door. In fact, from the look on his face, he probably didn't know whether to laugh or run away, but he is a polite gentleman and somehow managed to do neither. But it took him a minute to say something.

"I see you are, uh, ready, Ida," he said at last. "Let's go." He looked around, probably to make sure no one was watching who might see him walking down the hallway with me in my clown suit. Fortunately for both of us, the hallway was deserted.

"I hope you don't mind if Rose Kaplan comes along to watch," I said. "She's anxious to see how it goes, my riding the motorcycle."

"Uh, no, not at all, not at all." But he didn't sound like he meant it.

I put on a coat over my leather costume, to avoid at least a *bissel* of the embarrassment—to either of us—in case we did meet someone on our way out, which I'm sure Moishe appreciated. I carried with me the black shiny helmet with the orange stripes. I didn't want anyone should think we are being invaded from Mars.

On the way we stopped for Mrs. K, who wanted to see not how my riding went, but my not riding, if you know what I mean.

We did not in fact meet anyone on our way, *Got tsu danken*. When we entered the garage, all I could see were several rows of parked cars: black ones, silver ones, white ones. I wonder why I almost never see other colors on cars, like I remember when I was growing up—my father had one that was sort of white like cream on top and turquoise on the bottom. Now they all look the same, so it is hard to tell which is yours.

I was getting very warm in my leather costume and coat, so I took off the coat and handed it to Mrs. K, who from the look on her face seemed to be enjoying this much more than I was. We walked down an aisle facing the fronts of one of the rows of cars. I had a feeling like they were all staring at me with their big round glass eyes. I couldn't blame them, me looking like a cross between, you'll excuse the expression, a *nafkeh*—a whore—and a bad advertisement for a zipper company.

We reached the end of the aisle and turned a corner, and there it was: the big black motorcycle.

Even though I was not planning to get on that machine, it scared me just to look at it so closely. It looked like someone had stolen the body from one of the cars we had just passed and left only the big engine, one eye, and two of its wheels, with a little seat perched on top. On its side was its name, in fancy letters, "Harley Davidson." Of Mr. Davidson I have heard. It seemed to be sleeping, and I was very glad it was going to stay that way!

"I'll open the garage door," Moishe said. He went

over to the opposite wall and pressed a button. Immediately the big metal garage door began to roll itself up, making a loud clattering sound. "If you ladies will wait over there for a minute," Moishe shouted over the noise while gesturing to an open space just outside of the door, "I'll start the engine and bring the bike outside. It can be a bit loud when it starts up in here."

Mrs. K and I obeyed Moishe's instructions, although we had no fear that the noise would be too loud, unless you count whatever screams of frustration we might hear from poor Moishe when he was unable to make the machine start.

We watched as Moishe returned to the motorcycle. First he put on his helmet, with the part that goes over his face pushed up, so he could see what he was doing. He climbed on the seat and put his hands on the ends of the handlebars. He looked like a child trying to ride his father's bicycle, and I admit I felt sorry for him at that moment and a little bit guilty for having put him in such an embarrassing position. But as Mrs. K pointed out, it had to be done for his sake and ours, not to mention Little Moishe's. We waited for him to put his foot on the kick starter, wherever that was, and try to start the engine.

But he didn't put his foot anywhere special. He just pressed some kind of button on the handlebar and—*Oy Gotenu*—suddenly there was a deafening roar.

The big black motorcycle had come to life!

****

Mrs. K and I looked at each other in horror. This was not what was supposed to happen. Of course, we were puzzled as to how Moishe had managed to start the motor with only the pressing of a button. Only later did we learn that the previous afternoon, having made the "date" with me and well aware he could not start the motorcycle with the kick starter, Moishe had had the electric starter fixed. Who knew he was so efficient?

We now were like those people who stand and watch an accident scene. We watched and waited to see whether Moishe, now that he had the motor running, could move the heavy machine off its stand and actually drive it. Needless to say, we were very much hoping he could not, because if he was able to drive it out of the garage…well, it was not something I wished to think about.

It was obvious that before Moishe could get the motorcycle going, like a bicycle it had to be taken off the dingus that holds it up, the kickstand. This is the thing that keeps it from falling over, since it has only the two wheels. And Little Moishe had assured Mrs. K that his father would never be able to do this, as it was much too heavy for him. But then, the same genius had told us that Moishe would never be able to start it in the first place.

Wrong again.

It is true Moishe pushed as hard as he could and the motorcycle did not budge. Oh, it rocked back and forth a little, but that was all. Mrs. K and I were much relieved to see this, and we were about to go inside and thank Moishe for the invitation when he called out to us.

"Would you ladies mind stepping back in here for a moment?"

We looked at each other and Mrs. K shrugged her shoulders, but we walked back to the parking place where Moishe was sitting on the motorcycle, which, after its roar of waking up, was going "burble-burble-burble" very politely.

When we reached Moishe, he said, "I know it's a lot

to ask of you ladies, but I'm having a little trouble getting the bike off its stand. Would you mind giving me a hand?"

Again Mrs. K and I exchanged puzzled looks. "Us? What is it you want us to do?" Mrs. K asked.

"Oh, just get on either side and grab hold of that bar"—indicating a shiny silver tube that looked like a handle of some kind on the back of the seat—"and when I say, lean forward and pull."

What to do? It was like a condemned prisoner being asked to help build the gallows on which he will be hung. He can refuse, but it will probably only delay the execution. No doubt if we decline to help, Moishe just finds someone else to give him a push. So reluctantly I took hold of the shiny bar and Mrs. K did the same, and when Moishe said "Now," we pulled.

I suppose the weight of all of us leaning on Mr. Davidson was enough to make him move, because suddenly he was rolling forward with Motorcycle Moishe on his back and driving.

Of course, I was not yet sitting on the machine, but was still safely watching as it took Moishe out the door into the sunshine.

Zie gezunt, I am thinking. Go and be well. Just do not come back for me!

I would like to say that Moishe rode off on Mr. Davidson and that was the last of him we saw that day. I would like to, but I cannot, because as soon as he was outside and in the driveway of the Home, Moishe stopped the motorcycle. This created another problem for him. Because the heavy machine was not on its little kickstand, Moishe had to hold it up while remaining on the seat. We could see it start to tip over to the left, then to the right, but finally Moishe got it balanced in between. He then looked back at me and Mrs. K and called out the words I most did not want to hear:

"Okay, Ida. You can get on now."

I looked at Mrs. K and said to her, "Rose, he expects me to get on that machine. What do I do now? I cannot tell him now that I only agreed to come riding with him because we assumed he would never get the machine started or off its stand, much less out of the garage."

"No, Ida, I see what you mean. And I feel responsible for putting you in this situation, and for assuming that what Little Moishe said about his father not being able to drive the motorcycle was true. But I'm afraid you have now only two choices: You can tell Moishe the truth, and that includes the fact that it was all my idea and you never intended to ride with him, or you can walk out there and get on the motorcycle. I wish there was a third choice, but I do not see one."

Maybe if we had had more time we could have come up with another plan. Like I suddenly have a fainting spell and have to be carried back inside. But neither I nor Mrs. K, who as I have said thinks much more quickly than I do, thought of that at the time. We saw only the two choices: Confess or ride.

Well, somehow I couldn't tell Moishe, who is a *mensch*, though a *meshuggeneh* one, the truth, even if it was not my idea. I had to get on the motorcycle.

Mrs. K squeezed my hand, and I walked toward the open garage door, Moishe still looking back as he held up the motorcycle. You remember what I said about the condemned prisoner building his own gallows? Well, now I felt like I was about to put my head into the noose, walking the "last mile," as they say. And in this ridiculous leather costume, yet, complete with space helmet.

I was angry with myself for having put myself in such a terrible situation. I was even angry, quite unreasonably I know, at Mrs. K for having advised me to do it. But fortunately I had forgotten one very important thing: When it comes to anything that requires what you would call athletic ability, I am a real *klutz*. A little awkward. Even in school as a child, I was never very good at sports. Because I now play games like bridge or canasta instead of hopscotch or basketball, being a *klutz* has been only a mild nuisance to me. But I never thought it would actually become a benefit!

Nevertheless, that is exactly what happened. I gathered my courage and walked up to the motorcycle, which Moishe was holding upright with obvious difficulty as it burbled and chugged, no doubt wanting to be unleashed and allowed to run.

"What should I do?" I asked Moishe, I never having gotten onto such a beast before.

"Just grab the chrome bar behind my seat, put your right foot on the little step there, and swing your left leg over." Then he added reassuringly with a smile, "It's easy, just take your time."

Nu, time was not my problem. With the grabbing and the putting I had no difficulty. But with the swinging, that was another story altogether. I don't know whether I could have made a successful sitting on the seat if I hadn't been wearing that heavy leather jacket and chaps, not to mention the big space helmet with the orange stripe. Maybe yes, maybe no. What I do know is that, combined with my bursitis and my being a *klutz*, instead of my left foot swinging over to the other side of the motorcycle, it instead struck the big animal in the *tuchis*, if you know what I mean. Apparently that tipped it sideways just enough so that it began to fall and Moishe, who was only barely keeping it upright in the first place, was unable to stop it falling completely over. It was a little like you see in those movie scenes where everything slows down like it is happening underwater, and maybe two lovers are floating across a meadow toward each other.

I had no idea Moishe, at his age, could jump that far that fast! But jump he did, and just in time, because had he not, Mr. Harley Davidson would surely have fallen right on top of him. As it was, he missed Moishe by a good six inches as the big machine went crashing to the ground. And there it lay, like a wounded animal, still burbling and growling, but—more like an upside-down turtle—unable to get up on its own. I of course lost my balance and ended up *kop* over *tuchis*—head over behind—on the other side of the machine. *Oy gevalt*, what a mess!

Mrs. K, who had watched the entire scene unfold, came running over to see if we were hurt. I seemed to be only a little shaken up, saved from any real damage by being completely covered from head to foot in armor that would have made proud a knight by King Arthur. Now I know why they wear the black leather and the shiny helmet.

But I still cannot understand about the zippers.

Now you might think that this that I have described to you was a real *brokh*, a total disaster. But in fact, as I said, it turned out to be a stroke of good fortune, thanks to Mrs. K. My first thought, after checking to see that I was still in one piece, was to blame Moishe for the silly idea, in addition to Mrs. K for talking me into going along with it. But it was she who saw the possibility for making lemon pudding from lemons.

Seeing that I was unhurt, Mrs. K then rushed over to Moishe, who fortunately was hurt only in his pride, and apologized profusely on my behalf, as if the entire mess was my fault! I began to protest, as best I could from where I was sitting, but then I heard Moishe reply, and I understood.

"Oh, that's all right, Rose," says Moishe. "Riding a motorcycle is not for everyone, and of course Ida didn't mean to knock the bike over. I'm sure we would have had a wonderful ride together, but as it is, there doesn't seem to be any harm done, *Got tsu danken.*"

He then stood up, brushed himself off, and checked for any injuries. Finding none, he came around to where I was sitting on the ground and helped me to stand up. I too apologized for being such a *klutz* and knocking over his machine. "All my fault," I told him.

"Do not worry, Ida. I'm just glad you're all right," he said. "I never should have insisted you come for a ride." He then lowered his voice and continued, "To tell you the truth, Ida, I probably should not have been riding either. It's a long time since I was trying to handle such a large bike by myself, and, well, I think it's time I let my son do all the driving, and I shall continue to ride in back. I enjoy it very much, and he is strong like I used to be."

So somehow my pushing over Mr. Davidson convinced Moishe he should not try to drive motorcycles anymore, and my taking the blame for it let him save face.

So all is well that ends well; and all would have been

too, if Moishe had just not added one last sentence:
"I shall ask him to take you for a ride instead."

Chapter Twenty

I seem to have gotten a *bissel* far from Vera's murder, so let me bring you back to the evening before I had the encounter with Mr. Harley Davidson. After dinner, Mrs. K and I were watching a movie on her television. I think it was one of those they call "chick flicks," or something like that. The girl is going to marry some *shlemiel* until along comes this *mensch*, and she almost marries the *shlemiel* but at the last minute she goes for the nice boy instead, as we all knew she would. Anyway, we're watching this movie when there is a knocking on the door.

It was Fannie.

"I'm sorry to bother you," Fannie said, "but I was wondering whether you had heard anything further about, you know, about my sister's death."

"I assume you know about Daniel being arrested," Mrs. K said. By now I think everyone in the Home knew that.

"Yes, of course, and I've heard that Vera was poisoned in some way or other."

"In fact, she was given a medicine that when combined with what she was already taking—something starting with a 'Z,' I think—made her heart fail."

"I see. That's interesting. But that can't be the end of the matter. I mean, surely you don't think her own son…"

"No, of course not. Ida and I have talked with the police and we're doing what we can to find the real person responsible."

"And have you made any…any progress?"

Mrs. K looked at me, and I shrugged my shoulders a bit. How much, if anything, should we tell Fannie? The police said we should not discuss details with others. But after all, it was Fannie who first raised the alarm, and who asked Mrs. K to help. We should at least give her some idea of where things stand.

While I was thinking these things, so was Mrs. K. She obviously came to about the same conclusion as I did.

"Fannie, dear, the police still think that Daniel seemed to have a motive and opportunity to…to do it. But they're still nosing around, and we're trying to help them find someone else who is a more likely suspect."

"So do they have any other suspects?" Fannie asked.

"Yes and no. There were a few other people who entered Vera's room that day, such as the nurse who usually gives her a pill with lunch, and two people they have not identified who entered in the late afternoon."

"Two people."

"Yes, at least two." Obviously Mrs. K did not want to tell Fannie, or anyone else, that we had already guessed it was Rena and talked with her.

"Why would these people be going into my sister's room in the afternoon? Were they cleaners or something?"

"Possibly. Have you any idea who they might have been?"

Fannie appeared to think about this for a moment.

"No, other than the cleaning staff, and maybe a

nurse, I can't think of anyone. But if my sister was indeed poisoned, I don't see why it matters. She wouldn't have taken any medicine anyway."

Again we looked at each other with surprise.

"She wouldn't? How do you know this?"

"Because it was *Yom Kippur*, of course. All of her medicines were to be taken with food, and of course we fasted all day. She wouldn't take her medicines that morning from me, so I'm reasonably sure she wouldn't have taken them from anyone else until after sundown, after *Yom Kippur* was over."

This was something neither I nor Mrs. K had considered, and it was a big shock to us both.

"But Fannie," Mrs. K said, "you know that one is permitted to take medicine, even to eat, on *Yom Kippur* if it is necessary for one's health. Surely your sister knew that and didn't refuse her medicine."

"Yes, I know that, and I argued with her about it briefly, but she said she was feeling better and missing one day wouldn't matter. She was quite adamant about it. I even went to find Dr. Menschyk to ask him if it really was okay for her to miss a day of medicine, but I couldn't find him, so I left it at that and went to services. So you see, until sundown, no one could have given Vera any medicine, unless they somehow forced it on her."

"But of course then she would have told someone, certainly Daniel, what had happened," Mrs. K said. She sounded quite miserable, because of course if no one could have given Vera the wrong medicine until sundown when *Yom Kippur* ended, then the only person who could have given her the bad medicine was the one who came to her room after the Day of Atonement was over.

Only Daniel.

****

After Fannie left the room, Mrs. K and I sat and talked for a while about what we had learned from her. It was not a happy talk.

"First of all, I'm surprised that Vera would refuse to take her medicine on purely religious grounds," Mrs. K said. "She never struck me as that Orthodox to begin with, and in any event, we know that anyone needing to take medicine is excused from fasting on *Yom Kippur*. Surely she knew that too."

"Maybe not. And besides, isn't it true that people sometimes become much more religious when they have a life-threatening illness? But if she was being so strict about it, do you then think she also refused to take her pills from Daniel the evening before, on erev *Yom Kippur*? The Day of Atonement would have officially started then."

"We could ask Daniel, I suppose. But remember that he had to be at services himself by sundown, so he would likely have given her the medicine earlier that evening, before the beginning of the fast. And of course we all ate early so we could be finished before sundown."

"Hmm. That's true. So all we really know is that Vera refused to take her morning medicines. If someone tried to give her something later in the day, she may have refused, or maybe she was persuaded that it was in her best interest."

"*Gotteniu*! One way or the other, Ida, this makes it even harder to find a more likely suspect than Daniel."

So maybe we were on the wrong team after all?

Chapter Twenty-One

So Mrs. K and I are sitting reading in the lounge the next morning—you have noticed that we spend a lot of time in the lounge, but it really is the most comfortable place to read or sip our tea, or both together—when again I have the feeling someone is watching us.

This time I turned around quickly, or as quickly as a person built like me can turn, and I could swear I saw a man who had been standing behind a decorative screen—it hides a waste basket—quickly turn and walk away. I couldn't tell who it was, but from the little I could see from the back, I could say for certain was that he was short, heavyset, and balding. That describes a lot of people of my acquaintance.

"Excuse me a minute," I said to Mrs. K as I got to my feet. I didn't want to bother her with what was probably my overactive imagination, but I was sufficiently curious to do a tiny bit of investigating myself. I walked to the front desk and asked Joy Laetner, the morning receptionist, if someone of this description had come in recently.

"Sure did," Joy said. "I didn't recognize him, so I had him sign in." She indicated the sign-in list on the corner of the desk. I looked at it and there it was, on the last filled-in line, the name of the strange visitor:

"Fred Herrington."

****

That evening was the play to which Isaac Taubman had invited Mrs. K. It was Friday evening, the beginning of *Shabbos*, and ordinarily we would all be at services. But Mrs. K and I, as well as Taubman for that matter, are not so religious that we won't miss services if there is something else important to do.

Mrs. K and Taubman were to leave by taxi at about 7:30. At 7 o'clock she called me on the telephone and asked me to come over to her apartment. "I would like you should give me your opinion on something," she said.

I wondered on what my opinion was wanted, so I went right over. I knocked on Mrs. K's door and walked in, as I usually do. She was in her bedroom, standing in front of a full-length mirror.

"What do you think, Ida?" she said. "Is this the right thing for tonight?"

Now you can be sure this was not the first time Mrs. K had gone to a play in the evening. In fact, she and I frequently attended concerts or plays together, although we usually preferred afternoon matinees. She had never before asked my advice on what to wear.

I moved closer to get a better look at her dress. As I did, I sniffed a scent I didn't recognize.

"Rose, are you wearing a new perfume?" I asked.

"No, no, it's only some toilet water, and I've had it around for a long time. My daughter gave it to me. I just haven't worn it before." This would have been Mrs. K's daughter Rachel, who is married to a doctor.

"Well, it's quite pleasant. Not at all like the aftershave or cologne or whatever it is men sometimes wear. You almost need a gas mask to get near them."

Mrs. K laughed. "Yes, I often think they must take

179

a bath in it, or maybe apply it with a fire hose. Maybe they can't smell it themselves."

"Then they must have no sense of smell. But don't worry, what you are wearing is very nice."

"Thank you, Ida. And the dress?"

I looked at the pretty black dress with delicate flowers here and there. It really was quite becoming, which I told her. I hadn't seen it before.

"So you are ready for your date," I said. "It's been a while since you've been on one."

Mrs. K waved this off. "It's not a date, Ida," she said emphatically. "It's merely two friends going to a play. It's no different than when you and I do the same."

"Maybe," I said, "but unless that reporter at the gay restaurant was right in what he first assumed, the fact that I am a woman and Isaac is a man makes it different."

She laughed. "Let's not argue about it, Ida, because however you want to characterize it, it's still just two people going to a play. If the play is good, we shall have a good time. That's all."

A few minutes later, as she was ready to leave, she said, "I do feel bad for Karen, though. I think you were right, that she wanted Isaac to invite her, and perhaps she resents that he invited me instead."

"Oh, didn't I tell you? I saw Karen earlier this afternoon and she looked quite pleased. She told me that at the last minute Ben Lowenstein had asked her to accompany him to the play."

"Really? Lowenstein is, I think, the youngest man living here. Just in his sixties. And he's not so bad looking either."

"No, really quite handsome, I would say."

"And Karen is quite pretty herself and only a few

years older than Lowenstein. I'm not surprised she's pleased. I'm pleased too."

"So now you have, what do they call it, a clear field with Isaac Taubman, yes?" I couldn't resist asking.

Mrs. K blushed just a *bissel*. "I meant I was pleased for Karen. I already told you, this is not a date, it is just two friends attending a play. Perhaps you would like to come along as a chaperone?"

We both laughed at that. If a lady and a gentleman in their seventies require a chaperone to keep them out of trouble, the world has indeed turned upside down.

"I would go along and protect you from Taubman," I lied, "but as you know I'm leaving in the morning to visit Morty for the weekend and won't be available for this important duty. You will just have to behave yourselves on your own."

It was true that I would be visiting my son Morty and his family and staying overnight. I was looking forward to seeing my two grandchildren, who are already teenagers.

"I know, Ida," Mrs. K said. "And I'm sure you will have a wonderful time. And while you are gone, I intend to spend a lot of time thinking very hard about Daniel's situation. I'm sure there is something important we're missing. There must be. If not, then Daniel is the guilty one, and I continue to believe that is not possible. So I must find another solution that, although it may be improbable, is the truth."

And I was confident that she would discover the truth. But I was not as certain as she as to whether that truth would find Daniel to be innocent or guilty. *Chas v'cholileh*! God forbid.

Chapter Twenty-Two

I had a very nice time visiting Morty. He and his wife Joanne live in a spacious house in the suburbs, one of those newer kind that look like someone stuck two matzoh boxes together and surrounded it with a strip of *gehockteh leber*—chopped liver. Whatever happened to peaked roofs, bay windows, and pretty back gardens? *Nu*, it is their house, and they seem to like it.

Joanne, whose maiden name I believe was Livingston, is a very sweet girl. She is what's called a "Jew by choice," a convert, and she acts much like so many of the people I have known who have converted to Judaism: She is, if I may say so, "more Jewish" than many who were born that way. She is the one in the family who insists on celebrating all of the Jewish holidays and who supervised the children's Jewish education. She has been president of both their synagogue and the temple Sisterhood. She is active in Hadassah and other Jewish women's organizations. My friend Patricia Wilson, who is a Gentile, once told me it's the same when someone converts to Christianity. I remember her quoting someone who said that "there is no zealot like a convert." She said the best example was the Apostle Paul, of whom I have of course heard. I don't know in what religion Paul brought up his children.

Morty and Joanne have two children: Michael, who is fifteen, and Aviva, who is seventeen. Michael is fast becoming a man, and he is already as tall as his father. He is good at sports, I'm told, like playing football and baseball. And Aviva, she is growing up to be a real *krasavitseh*, a beautiful woman. They are good children, but like most teenagers these days, they seem always to have plugs in their ears, as if they're hard of hearing, with wires trailing down each side like thin *payess*, the long sideburns worn by orthodox Jews, and disappearing into their clothing. And of course there are the smarty telephones, like the one Sara gave to me. Only they don't seem to use them for making telephone calls, but only for sending messages with their thumbs and listening to music in those things in their ears. And to take pictures. Pictures of everything.

I had brought along my new telephone, and they tried to show me how to do the "texting." But my thumbs would not do what they were supposed to, and I usually ended up with words that looked like they were written in secret code. It used to be an insult to say someone was "all thumbs," but my grandchildren were writing messages so fast it looked like they were indeed all thumbs, and so I guess that phrase is now more of a compliment.

Nu, so of course the children were insisting on teaching me how to use my new telephone, even if my thumbs had to move much slower than theirs. They found it funny that I couldn't understand half the words they used in their messages, like "LOL" and "IMHO." They also taught me lots of other things I could do with my telephone, like taking pictures, including those "selfies" that Sara had mentioned, recording voices, and even making movies. They showed me how to put what are called "apps" on my phone, little pictures which

183

could do everything from reading those squares with the little squiggles you see everywhere to telling me how to get to Yahupitz by the shortest route. I didn't see when I would ever need all those gadgets—it was like one of those knives with a hundred blades, the ones from Switzerland, where you only use about two or three of the blades ninety-nine percent of the time—but I pretended like I was as excited about having them as they were to show me.

Sunday afternoon I returned to the Home. As soon as I had unpacked and settled myself, I telephoned Mrs. K, on my regular telephone with the cord attached, to see whether she had gotten any further in our investigation of Vera's death while I was gone. And to ask about her date with Taubman, of course.

"Yes, Ida," she said, "in fact there is much for me to tell you. Why don't you come over and I will tell you all about it."

That seemed like a good idea, and soon we were sitting in Mrs. K's living room sipping hot tea from Mrs. K's lovely bone china teacups—oolong, I think, which she had bought on our last shopping trip, as all we get at the Home is Mr. Lipton.

"So how was the play, and how was your date with Taubman?" I asked. First things first.

"I've told you it was not a date, just going to a play together. And it was very nice, thank you. The acting was quite good, and the surprise ending was, well, a surprise."

"And was Taubman a…a gentleman throughout?"

"He didn't make a pass at me, if that's what you mean. Really, Ida, we aren't sixteen years old anymore. You should not pretend we are."

"You do not have to be sixteen, or even sixty, to have a *kush*, a little smooch, with a handsome man. You are never too old, in my opinion."

Mrs. K sighed. "Yes, you're right, Ida. But in this case, there was no smooch, just maybe a polite squeeze of the hand when he took me to my door. But I will be honest: If he had tried a smooch, I would not have screamed for help or given him a *klap* on the *kop*. But he didn't, and that's just fine."

"And will you be going out with him again soon?" This was beginning to sound promising. Not that I was trying to make a marriage for Mrs. K—I'm not a *shadkhen*, a matchmaker—but only that it had been a long time since either of us had really socialized with a person of the opposite sex. Unless you consider my experience with Motorcycle Moishe socializing, and I would rather you did not.

Mrs. K smiled, a little like that smile on that Mona Lisa lady, as if there was a secret behind it. She said, "Let's just say he has asked if we might go together somewhere else in the future, and I have said yes. We shall leave it at that."

"*Mazel tov*. So now what is it you did while I was away?" I asked.

"First tell me about your visit. How are Morty and the family? The children are well?"

"Very well, thank you. The grandchildren are growing up so fast! And they know so much more— about everything—than we did at their age. It's a bit scary."

"I know what you mean. But that's just the way of the world now, I suppose."

"Yes, I suppose. Anyway, I learned more about

185

using my new telephone. And seeing everyone reminded me I must update my will. I haven't done so since Michael and Aviva were very little, and my lawyer warned me then to be sure to have it looked at every few years, because if the family situation changes....But enough about that. Tell me what you were up to."

"Well, it was a very eventful weekend. It began Saturday morning. When I was taking my vitamin pills." I have seen Mrs. K's assortment of vitamin pills, and they cover most of the alphabet. "I had this little idea, a—what do they call it, the fancy name—an epiphany. And the rest of the day I spent trying to follow this idea to see where it might take me."

"Following it how?"

"Oh, a lot of snooping. And questioning. First I had a long talk with Daniel."

"About what? About his mother?"

"No, not exactly. You might say it was a professional consultation. I wanted to know certain things about medicines."

"And then?"

"And then I telephoned to Inspector Corcoran. I didn't think he would be working on Saturday, but I took a chance and he was indeed in his office."

"What did you want from Corcoran?"

"Do you remember Hannah telling us about this cousin, Erik? And how she knew he was quite a heavy gentleman?"

"Yes, I think she said Vera had shown her an old picture of their family and he was in it. Wasn't that it?"

"Yes, that's right. What I wanted from Corcoran was that he should find out whether that picture was among Vera's possessions after her death."

"Wouldn't her family have taken all of her belongings by now?"

"Yes, you would think so. And I asked Daniel whether he had seen it. But he said he hadn't, and that the police were holding certain of Vera's things while they investigated, and they had not yet returned everything. So that's why I asked Corcoran if he had, or could locate, that picture."

"But he said we should not be asking any more questions, that we should stay out of the case. Was he willing to help you with this?"

"I will admit he was reluctant at first, but I think he realized he would not be doing his job properly if he didn't at least consider evidence that showed up after he already made an arrest, even if the police didn't themselves find that evidence."

"And he said…"

"He said he didn't know, that he didn't recall any photograph, but then he hadn't been looking for one. And once I described it to him, he said in light of the report of a heavyset man snooping around Vera's room that afternoon, and our telling him about the cousin, perhaps it would be a good idea to try to find a photograph of someone it might have been."

"I suppose they have gotten some kind of photograph of him from the prison? Don't they always take, what is it called, a 'mug shot' of new prisoners? At least that's what they do in the movies."

"Yes, I suppose so, but people look different in different situations, don't they? Would you have recognized yourself from the pictures they used to take for your driver's license? When you had one, that is?"

I laughed. "I see what you mean."

187

"And I wanted to see that photograph of Vera's family anyway. I thought it could be very useful."

"So Corcoran agreed it was a good idea to find the photograph?"

"Yes, although he didn't sound happy about it. He said he would see if they still had it. And frankly I didn't care why he thought it was a good idea, as long as he found it and let me see it."

"And did he find it?"

"I don't know yet. At least he hasn't told me so. But I'm hoping he will by tomorrow. If it is not with Daniel, and if Vera still had it—and that is a big if—it must be with the police."

"So, Rose, it sounds like you had a successful day of snooping. I am sorry I missed it."

"Don't worry, Ida. There is much more left to do."

And as I soon found out, there was.

Chapter Twenty-Three

On Monday morning, Mrs. K received a telephone call from Inspector Corcoran.

"Ida," she said when we met for breakfast, "he has found the photograph and we can come down to look at it if we wish."

"And do we wish?" I still was not sure why Mrs. K wanted to see that photograph.

"Well, yes, at least I do. Perhaps there is no need for you to come along if you have other things to do this morning."

As it happened, I did have an appointment with a podiatrist, who comes to the Home so we don't have to *shlep* downtown to his office. It's a little perk, as they say, of being old. So Mrs. K went to see the photograph by herself. I didn't mind, as I had no particular desire to see what this Erik looked like some years ago. When I asked Mrs. K why she wanted to, as usual she said she would tell me later, when she had more information. To be honest, I often have trouble following Mrs. K's reasons for some of the things she does, so I'm quite content to wait until she has finally figured something out and she explains to me at one time the whole *megillah*, the entire story, including the ending.

My appointment was over before noon—Dr. Simmons said the pain in my foot would go away if I put one of these curved doohickeys in my shoe—and by lunchtime Mrs. K was back. She seemed quite excited.

"It is as I thought," she said when we had been seated and served.

"And how is that?"

"I will explain later. Let's have our lunch in peace and not worry about Daniel or the police for now."

This seemed a good idea, especially as both Karen Friedlander and Isaac Taubman had just come to the table. Not only would it be impolite to ignore them, but what we had to discuss was not what one would call public information. And perhaps Mrs. K and Taubman would like to talk about their date-that-was-not-a-date. *Mazel tov*. Our discussion could wait.

About an hour later, someone knocked on my door just as I was finishing with the toilet. Have you noticed that you can go the whole day with no one knocking on your door or calling you on the telephone, but the five minutes you are on the toilet, the telephone will ring and the door will knock? At least I have a telephone extension in the bathroom, but I cannot open the front door from there. Maybe I should start to carry my smarty telephone into the bathroom; I have heard ladies in the public restrooms talking on their phones while on the toilet, as if they were sitting in their living rooms at home. It's what they call multitasking, I think.

Anyway, I put myself together and hurried to the door. It was Mrs. K, and she had a worried expression on her face.

She came in and sat down on the sofa. She looked quite serious.

"So, Ida," she said, "we are now getting to what you might call the heart of the matter. But I still need certain information before I know if I am, as you put it the other day, barking at the wrong tree."

Usually if Mrs. K is barking at a tree, it turns out to be the right one. But there is always an exception possible.

"And there is a problem finding this information?"

"I think there will be. Let's look at the possibilities."

I asked Mrs. K to wait while I made some tea and we could relax a little. She seemed like she could use it.

It took me only a few minutes to boil the water and make the tea, and soon we were sipping and Mrs. K looked much more relaxed than she did when she knocked on the door.

"So, Rose. Perhaps you should start at the beginning. Otherwise I will be getting confused."

Mrs. K put down her teacup and cleared her throat.

"Ida, do you remember I said that on Saturday morning I had a little idea?"

"Yes, certainly I remember. It was while you were brushing your teeth, wasn't it?"

"Actually, it was while I was taking my vitamins, but that's close enough. And I spent a great deal of time thinking and, as I told you, asking questions of Daniel and Inspector Corcoran. And now I have seen the photograph, and things are beginning to fall into place. I am seeing possibilities that I did not see before, although some of them might seem quite improbable."

This reminded me of the important lesson of Mr. Sherlock Holmes that Mrs. K is fond of quoting: "When you eliminate what is impossible, what is left over must be the truth, no matter how *meshugge* it might seem." I mentioned this to Mrs. K.

"I'm pleased that you see where I'm going with this," she said. "I have eliminated what at least I consider impossible, and I'm trying not to let the fact that some more possible solution is—what is the expression—is a long shot, keep me from considering it."

"So what is the impossible, and when we take it out, what is left?"

"Yes, isn't that what they call the sixty-four dollar question? What could and could not have happened, I've been asking myself, given what we know and what Inspector Corcoran has told us?"

"And did you now come to a conclusion?" I could tell Mrs. K was excited, like a hunting dog that is getting near the rabbit it has been following. I also know that at such a time, she is more interested in pouncing on the rabbit than stopping to explain where she thinks it is hiding.

So I was not surprised or disturbed when she answered, "Not yet, but I'm getting there. I still need to find a couple of important pieces to the puzzle. They are related to the two medicines that we were told were together responsible for Vera's death. I can think of only two, or maybe three, ways to get this information."

"And they are…"

"Well, the easiest way would be to get certain medical records. I was going to ask Inspector Corcoran for another favor, that he should get these records for me."

"I don't know, Rose," I said. "Medical records? They are extremely confidential, aren't they? I remember Morty telling me that when Joanne was in the hospital with some kind of infection, they wouldn't tell him anything about her condition, even though he's her husband, until she signed some kind of paper saying it was okay he should know. So if a husband cannot even find out about his sick wife…"

"Yes, exactly. That's why I hope Corcoran will help. The police can get information that we cannot."

"But even if they can, will they give it to you? You are not the police." It is true that once before, during that matter of the matzoh balls, Mrs. K had been able to obtain information from the police records of certain residents of the Home, and perhaps she was thinking she could do so again. But that time she had persuaded Isaac Taubman to ask his son Benjamin, who is a policeman, to get the information for her as a big favor. Benjamin could have lost his job if his superiors had found out. I reminded Mrs. K of this, and she agreed she could not ask such a favor again. And Corcoran would be a lot harder to persuade than Isaac Taubman!

Mrs. K thought about this problem for a long time, sipping her tea and looking somewhere far away. Finally, she said, "Yes, you're right. It probably isn't even worth asking Corcoran. It would not be proper for him to do this for me, and besides, he's already been very helpful about the photograph and I don't want to become a *nudge*, a nuisance. So that takes me to the second possible way to get the information.…" Her voice trailed off.

Mrs. K sounded even less enthusiastic about this choice than she had about the police.

"It would be a much more unorthodox method. One we used in the past, although very…very reluctantly." It sounded from her voice like she was even reluctant to mention it to me.

For a moment I couldn't understand to what Mrs. K might be referring. And then suddenly I had my own epiphany, or whatever it is. Or at least one of those light bulbs went on over my head for a change.

"You don't mean Sara's friend Florence, do you? Florence the lady burglar? Whose telephone Sara gave me?" I was hoping the answer was no, but I was pretty sure it was yes.

It was.

"I'm afraid so. Do you think it's possible she would do another big favor for us?"

"You mean enter a room again and look for, or at, something?" This was what the lady burglar had done for us once before. But it had not gone well.

"Yes, something like that. Do we dare ask her again?"

I thought about this for a moment. I answered reluctantly.

"To be honest, I don't think so. First of all, the last time it was you yourself who was, shall we say, in the soup. Florence did this as a favor to Sara, because I am Sara's aunt and you are my best friend. It is maybe too much to ask that she do it again, and this time for Daniel, who is not even related to you or me and a stranger to Sara." I knew that, as far as Mrs. K was concerned, she felt as close to Daniel as one can without being actually related, as I have already explained. But this would not be apparent to Sara's friend.

Mrs. K nodded, and I continued.

"There is also the fact that things did not work out exactly as they were planned the last time. We all survived, but I still sometimes have nightmares about it. So that is another reason I would be reluctant to ask her again."

"Yes, you're right, Ida," Mrs. K said. "We shall put that idea aside for the moment. But I still would like to speak with your niece Sara."

"Not about the lady burglar?"

"No, something else. I would like to ask a question of that lawyer she used to work for, what was his name?"

"Farraday, I think. Why do you need a lawyer? Are you in some kind of legal trouble?" This was a new development. I hadn't heard of any problem with the law Mrs. K was having.

She laughed. "No, Ida, I just wanted to ask something about a will."

I was relieved. "About updating your will?"

"Uh, something like that, yes."

"This is a good idea, Rose. I have to do the same," I said. "As I think I told you, it occurred to me when I was visiting Morty and seeing how quickly his children are growing up that I hadn't looked at my will in many years. Sara told me more than once—I think she knew as much about these things as Farraday did—that when there is a change in the family, who gets what in your estate can change too, so it's important to keep your will up to date."

"Yes, that's right, of course."

"I'll give you Sara's telephone number and you can ask her. I'm sure she will be glad to help. Maybe she can answer your question herself. As I said, after working for Mr. Farraday for many years, she learned quite a bit about his business. He even wanted to send her to school to become a—what is it called—a paralegal, I think it is. But she then got that inheritance and decided she would retire from working for a while."

"Yes, maybe she can answer my questions; that would be much easier. Thank you, Ida, I shall call her later."

"So back to your medical question. Is there any other way to get the information you need?"

"Yes, there is one more possibility. I shall see if Daniel can help with this. He may not be able or willing to, but I really won't know until I ask him."

And that is where we left it. I could tell Mrs. K was getting close to the end of the hunt for Vera's killer. I was somehow sure it would either be whoever it was she was now concentrating on, or it would be the only other alternative.

That would, of course, be Daniel.

Chapter Twenty-Four

On Tuesday morning after breakfast, Mrs. K and I went to see Daniel again. He was still looking gloomy, and who would not? The trout was still in the milk, as Mr. Thoreau apparently would say, and so far we had not been able to remove it.

"Don't worry, Daniel," Mrs. K told him. "I'm working on an idea that I hope will make everything much clearer. But I shall need your help again."

"Of course, I'll do whatever I can," he said.

"Good. I assume your pharmacy keeps records of who is prescribed what medicines, yes?"

"Well, yes, we do have that on our computer."

"So you could look up, say, whether last week or last month I was prescribed some particular drug."

"Yes, we can do that. Provided you purchased it there, of course."

"Ah. And what if I purchased it at another Buy & Save Drug Mart, but in some other city?"

"Hmm. I think it wouldn't matter, now that all the stores are linked by the same computer network."

"This network—can you get to it here? I mean, from home, if you are not back at the pharmacy?"

"Well, yes, I can still log in. I've had to do it from time to time."

"Good. And finally, how far back does this computer record go? More than, say, one year?"

Daniel thought for a minute. "I'm not certain, but I think the company policy is to keep records for at least seven, or maybe it's ten, years. Just in case of lawsuits and such. You know, if someone claims they were harmed by a particular drug, that sort of thing. So did you want me to find out what drugs my mother was taking? I thought the police already knew that from her doctor."

"It is something like that. But another person."

Daniel looked almost shocked by the suggestion.

"I can't do that, Rose. You must know that those records are confidential. It's against the law, as well as against company policy."

Mrs. K took Daniel's hand and, like a mother enlightening her son to the ways of the world, she patiently explained, "Daniel dear, I know you are a good person, an ethical person, and you would not violate either the law or your conscience for anything. We saw that when it came to the autopsy and the conflict with *Halacha*, with Jewish law. Now we seem to have a little conflict with the company rules."

"Not just company rules, Rose. As I said, it's also against the law. And while you convinced me there was an exception to the prohibition on autopsies in mother's case, I don't know of any exception to the confidentiality law that doesn't involve some kind of subpoena or other legal procedure."

Mrs. K was still patient, still like a mother to a son. "Yes, I understand. And I am as much a law-abiding person as are you. But in this case it's not a matter of your avoiding a little break in the law; it's a matter of your avoiding spending the rest of your life in prison. I would not ask you to do this if it were not the best— maybe the only—way I know to get this vital information."

Daniel lapsed into silence, looking troubled, as anyone would be. He stared down at his lap, in which his hands were folded, his knuckles white. Finally he looked up and said, "I'll think it over tonight and let you know tomorrow, is that okay?"

"Certainly," Mrs. K said. "Call me in the morning."

And that was how we left Daniel, just as gloomy as we found him, or maybe more so. Mrs. K didn't look much happier, and I couldn't blame her. She is not just law-abiding, like she said to Daniel. She is a person who, if a pay telephone accidentally gave her quarter back, she would mail it to the company. If there still were any pay telephones.

"I hope Daniel will agree to do this," Mrs. K said to me on our way out of the store. "If not, I may be out of ideas.

"And Daniel might be out of luck."

****

Back at the Home, Mrs. K and I went to our respective apartments to freshen up. According to what Mrs. K told me later, this is what happened next:

There was a knock on her door, quite a heavy knock. She opened the door, and there in front of her was a large man. "Like one of those football players, only older," she said. It was a little intimidating, and she is not a timid woman.

"Are you the lady who's asking all the questions about Vera Gold's death?" he said. It was hard to tell from his manner whether these words were a simple inquiry or some kind of an implied threat.

"I guess you could say that," Mrs. K replied. She could hardly deny it. "Why do you want to know?"

"I'm Fred Herrington."

Now at least she could start to put two and two together, although what they would add up to was not yet clear.

"You are the man who used to live with Vera?"

"That's right. Can I come in?"

She let him in. *Nu*, she couldn't just leave him standing in the hallway, could she? And besides, she naturally was curious as to not only why he was there, but also where he might fit into the puzzle we were still trying to work out.

Mrs. K showed Mr. Herrington into the living room, where he sat on the sofa, taking up more than his share of the cushions. She offered him tea. "No, thank you," he said, in a tone of voice that seemed to say, "I am here on serious business, not to drink tea."

"Mrs. Kaplan," he said, speaking slowly, when she had seated herself across from him, "I have a confession. I'm the one who…"

Before he could finish his sentence, Mrs. K jumped in with "Who killed Vera?" I think it was because she was so focused on that question, and here she might just have the answer handed to her, so to speak.

No such luck. "No, no," he said, laughing. He apparently looked much less threatening when he laughed. "Where did you get that idea?"

"I apologize. Please go on. To what do you want to confess?"

"That I've been kind of watching you the last few days. One time I think your friend noticed me, but I managed to disappear before she caught up with me."

"And why would you be watching me? Am I that interesting?"

Again he laughed. "No, no. I mean I'm sure you are an interesting person, but I'm afraid I tend to be somewhat…somewhat shy, I guess you'd say, around strangers, especially in public. I've wanted to talk with you, but I didn't want to just barge in on your conversation with your friend, I wanted to talk with you alone, and…well, I finally decided to come here, in private, instead."

"I see. Ida will be glad to know this. And now that the 'confession' is out of the way, what did you want to talk to me about?"

"About Vera, of course. I received a letter from an attorney saying she had passed away and that I was to receive something in her will. I had lost touch with her a few years ago, and this was the first I knew of her death."

"I imagine it was something of a shock to you, even if you had not seen her in a while. You had not been to see her at the Home before receiving this letter?"

"No. As I said, I hadn't seen her in quite a while."

"Did you…did you part on good terms?"

"Pretty good. It was what you might call by mutual agreement. Vera was becoming increasingly, well, difficult to live with. And I suppose I cramped her style a bit, being as nonsocial as I am. Vera always liked to be out and about. This was before she became ill, of course."

"Yes. But I still don't see why you were so anxious to talk with me, rather than the lawyer, or her son, Daniel."

"Daniel and I didn't…get along very well. We didn't agree on what was in Vera's best interests, I guess. I did go and see the lawyer, and he told me that the police were investigating Vera's death as a murder. That was a shock, I can tell you. And he said they had arrested Daniel. That was even more of a shock."

"To us also," Mrs. K said.

"Anyway, I wanted more information than the lawyer had, so I came here to the Home to find it."

"And why not to the police?"

Mr. Herrington looked a little uncomfortable. He said, "I…I've had some run-ins with the police in the past, and I try to keep my distance from them."

"So how did you know to look for me?"

He laughed. "Oh, it seems everyone here knows you're investigating Vera's death, trying to clear Daniel's name. Isn't that right?"

"I suppose so, yes. And to be honest, you are on my list of suspects."

Herrington looked quite surprised. "Me? Why me?"

"Well, we didn't know on what terms you parted from Vera. And there is the inheritance, isn't there?"

Another laugh. "Oh, that. I told the lawyer I was renouncing the gift in the will. I don't need the money, and whoever is next on the list probably does."

Mrs. K was, of course, surprised by this new information. She and Herrington talked about Vera and the investigation—the parts she could talk about publicly, of course—for quite a while. He even accepted another offer of tea before he left, having learned what he came to find out.

After I rejoined Mrs. K in the lounge and she described her meeting with Herrington, there was only one more thing to do:

Cross Fred Herrington off our list.

****

When we returned from breakfast the next day, there

was a message that Daniel had called. It said simply, "I'll do it. Give me a call. DG."

A large sigh of relief Mrs. K gave when she read this. "We are still in the game, Ida," she said. "Let's get this done before Daniel changes his mind. And before I do."

And that is what we did. Mrs. K telephoned Daniel and told him what she wanted him to look up. He agreed and said he would get back to her within an hour.

Daniel did call Mrs. K back about an hour later, and after hanging up the telephone, she turned to me looking more pleased than I had seen her since the evening of her date—or whatever it was—with Isaac Taubman.

"Ida, I think we are on the right track this time. There remains only one more thing I must do before we can go to see Inspector Corcoran with our information. And for that I must borrow your new telephone, the one Sara gave you."

"My telephone? What has that to do with anything? Of course you may borrow it, but…"

She laughed. "I apologize, Ida. I haven't been explaining things very well the last few days, have I? It's just that until I'm sure of something, I'm reluctant to go out on a limb, to tell even you what I'm thinking. Especially when it concerns other people. But now let me tell you exactly what I'm thinking, and you can tell me whether I'm on the right track or just totally *meshugge*."

So finally I was learning what all this gathering of information was for. Mrs. K began with her vitamin pill "epiphany" and explained all the steps in her reasoning. I must say, although I have often been impressed with how Mrs. K's mind works, this was the most impressive of all. And maybe the most surprising.

Unless, of course, it turned out to be wrong. And to be perfectly honest, I thought it had about the same chance of being right as being wrong. And that could be a disaster, because Mrs. K seemed to be putting all her eggs in the same carton.

What a mess if it tipped over…

****

I went to my apartment and got my new smarty telephone and handed it to Mrs. K. I then went over with her all of the instructions my grandchildren had given me, at least the ones I could still remember. She thanked me, put the telephone in her pocket, and said she now had a very important visit to make, and to wish her luck. I did, and then she was gone.

I had a feeling the next time I spoke with her, we would know all there was to know.

And I was right.

Chapter Twenty-Five

"Ida, we must go to see Inspector Corcoran right away. There is no time to lose."

Mrs. K had returned from wherever she had gone, and from the look on her face it had not been a pleasant experience. She also looked like she had been running, or at least moving more quickly than she is used to, which is not very quickly at all. She was out of breath.

She sat on the nearest chair while I dialed the number of the police department. A minute later I was talking with Inspector Corcoran. But I had hardly gotten past "hello" when Mrs. K got up and took from me the receiver.

"Inspector Corcoran, is that you?" she said. Her side of the conversation then went this way:

"I am fine, thank you. But I must see you right away." She looked over at me. "Ida and I.

"No, it cannot wait. I know who killed Vera Gold. And they know I know. I need to explain it to you as soon as possible.

"Yes, we can be there in half an hour. Yes, I understand. We are leaving now."

She hung up the telephone.

"Now?" I said. "We are going to see him now?"

"Yes. Get your coat. I shall hurry down to the front desk and ask for a taxi."

Mrs. K walked quickly to the front door. But before

she could open it, someone on the other side began pounding on it. *Oy*, such a *tummel*! I reached past Mrs. K to open it, but she grasped my arm and stopped me. The loud knocking continued.

"We cannot go that way," Mrs. K said, pushing me back from the door.

"But you know there is no other way out, except the back window...."

I suddenly had a vision of another time, another window, when we needed to get into an apartment at the Home to find important evidence. Getting Mrs. K through that window, from *bristen* at one end to *tuchis* at the other, was like pushing two pounds of chopped liver into a one pound jar.

"No, Rose," I said, "we are not climbing through another window."

But she was not listening. She was already in my bedroom, opening the window as wide as it would go. She pulled her skirt partway up so she could step out. The pounding on the door was accompanied now by a rattling of the handle.

"Remember last time…" I said.

"Last time we were climbing in. Now we are climbing out. It is different."

But just then the pounding and rattling stopped, and we heard someone walking rapidly away.

"Quick, Ida," Mrs. K said, "look to see if there is still anyone in the hallway."

I went back to the door and looked through the peephole. Seeing nothing, I opened the door only a crack, and I could still see no one in either direction. I reported this to Mrs. K.

"Then we must quickly go to the front desk and find

a taxi," she said, straightening her skirt and pushing me out the door ahead of her.

I won't say Mrs. K ran down the hallway, but she moved as fast as I could remember seeing her move, at least since the time that awful little Weinstein boy put his pet lizard down her dress. All the time she kept looking back, I'm sure not to see if I was following her—she knew I was—but to see if anyone else was. And just as we approached the lobby, someone did come running toward us—I couldn't tell who it was—but they stopped when we reached the lobby, in which were many residents sitting and conversing with friends or relatives. We quickly walked up to the front desk.

Out of breath and panting a bit, Mrs. K asked Joy Laetner, the receptionist on duty, to call us a taxi, and to hurry. "It is a matter of life and death," she said, exaggerating just a little, although perhaps not. Joy probably thought she was a little *meshuggeneh,* but being used to dealing with residents who are a bit *farmisht,* befuddled, she calmly said, "No need, Rose. That taxi out there just brought the Winterfelts home. If you hurry, you can catch him before he leaves."

Hurry we did.

****

I was tempted to ask Mrs. K for details as we rode, but she didn't seem in the mood—or to have the breath—to explain right then; and besides, I knew I would be hearing the whole story—at least the parts I didn't already know—very soon.

We arrived at the police headquarters and Mrs. K gave the taxi driver one of the senior citizen vouchers that we use—it gives us a nice discount—and we entered the building. We gave our names at the security desk and soon we were in the elevator and then sitting again in front of Inspector Corcoran's desk. Sitting at the end of the desk, notebook in his hand, was Jenkins. He did not look amused, although I'll admit he was not quite as sour-looking as I had seen him in the past. I was wishing we had brought some *mandelbrot* with us; maybe he would actually be smiling again.

Corcoran closed the door, then turned and looked at us. "Well, ladies," he said, "while I know I said you should keep your eyes and ears open and learn what you could, I didn't expect you to solve the case for us. Again. But it sounds like that's what you've done." His tone of voice was that of someone who is not quite sure whether he is consulting an expert or humoring a child. He obviously was prepared to do either.

He went to his desk and sat down in the big chair facing us.

"Okay, let's hear what you have to say. I can guess that you have not only discovered the real culprit, but that person is not Daniel Gold. Am I right?"

"Yes," Mrs. K said, "you are right." Now that she was back in her element, so to speak, back in her role of detective, she sounded no longer excited, but just confident. She spoke slowly and deliberately, as if considering her words carefully.

"You already know about the case up to about a week ago. Daniel has the motive and the opportunity. Vera was killed by two medicines working together, both of which had to be administered late in the afternoon of *Yom Kippur* or just after it ended. Daniel was the only person you had identified who was definitely with his mother, Vera, at the time and had a chance to give her both those medicines. Am I correct so far?"

Corcoran nodded. So did Jenkins. Mrs. K continued:

"Just like you, Ida and I concentrated on finding someone who was in Vera's room at that crucial time, who could have given her the bad medicine, and of course who had a motive to kill her. There seemed to be several people who in some way fit that description: a resident, who we think was Rena Shapiro; a cousin who Vera had helped send to jail and was now free; certain employees Vera had wronged; a former lover; and maybe others. But even if these individuals had been present at the right time, it did not seem likely that they either would have known what medicine to mix with the other to kill Vera, or would have been able to make her take it. If they had wanted to kill Vera, they could easily have smothered her with a pillow, as Rena admitted to us she had thought to do."

Here Jenkins stopped writing and spoke up, seeming somewhat startled.

"Hold on. You mean this Rena…"—consulting his notes—"Rena Shapiro admitted she was in the room and tried to kill Mrs. Gold.…"

"I did not say she tried, just that she said she had considered it."

"Nevertheless," Jenkins persisted, "why didn't you report that to us? Just because she says she didn't kill her…"

Corcoran placed a hand on Jenkins' arm, though gently. "Let's come back to that later, Martin, shall we?" You know, this was the first time I had heard Jenkins' first name. I remember thinking it somehow didn't seem to fit him. "I've learned in the past it's best to let Mrs. Kaplan tell her whole story. Then we can discuss what she did or didn't do."

Jenkins nodded, but he didn't look happy. Like a large dog who has been barking at the stranger but is restrained by his master from taking a bite out of him.

"Go on, please, Mrs. Kaplan," Corcoran said. "You were saying none of these people was likely to have administered the sibutramine. I agree. What then?"

"Then we seemed to be at a stone wall. Only Daniel fit the requirements. Why? Because of the time frame we were forced to accept. If we could, shall we say, expand that time frame, it would include many more possible suspects, would it not?"

"I suppose it would. If it could be expanded, as you say. But our doctors say…"

"Yes, yes, I know what they say. And I had no answer for that. Not until last Saturday morning."

"And what happened last Saturday morning?"

"I took my vitamin pills. Or rather my vitamin capsules."

"And that gave you extra energy to solve the case?" said Jenkins. I think I detected a bit of a smirk in his voice.

Mrs. K and Corcoran both gave Jenkins a very nasty look. Personally I thought it was funny, but I was afraid to laugh.

"No," Mrs. K said, "what it gave me was an idea. An epiphany, we called it."

"Which was?" Corcoran said.

"Which was that my vitamin C capsule would be a perfect way to commit this crime."

"With vitamin C? Vitamin C is perfectly harmless," said Jenkins.

"Of course it is," Mrs. K said. "But it comes in what they call a time-release capsule."

210

Corcoran suddenly looked more interested. "Okay, I see where you're going with this. You think someone could have taken such a capsule, emptied it out, and filled it with the sibutramine, which would then still be in Mrs. Gold's system later in the day when she took her usual dose of ziprasidone." I don't know how he was remembering those long names. I guess he had been thinking about the case a lot.

"Well, not exactly," Mrs. K said. "I suppose that's possible—and to be honest it's the first thing that occurred to me—but I'm not sure the process is that simple. Nevertheless, these time-release capsules got me thinking that there are other ways to accomplish the same thing, to give someone medicine at one time, and have it take effect later."

"And that is…"

"It's really quite simple. I give you a pill and tell you to take it later."

Corcoran and Jenkins both looked thoughtful. Corcoran said, "Yes, I suppose that's quite possible…."

"It is," said Mrs. K. "And as soon as I realized it, I had very many more possible suspects with an opportunity. I mean, if I could think of this, no doubt whoever killed Vera could think of it too." With this I would have disagreed, since Mrs. K thinks so much better than most people. "But which ones had a motive?"

Corcoran was following the story very closely now. "And did you find any such motives?"

"Not at first. That is, no more than we had already known about and dismissed. But then I suddenly realized that perhaps we were asking ourselves the wrong question."

"What do you mean, the wrong question? Isn't the

question who had a reason to kill Mrs. Gold? Or at least who would benefit from her death?"

"Yes and no. Those are, of course, important questions. But what we had not really asked ourselves is this: If the way Vera Gold was killed seemed to point only to one person, to Daniel, her son, who would benefit if Vera were dead and Daniel was convicted of the murder?"

There was silence in the room. It seemed like everyone there, including Jenkins, was thinking about this new question, turning it over in their minds, wondering whether the answer might be different from the answer to the earlier question.

Corcoran was the first to speak up. "I take it, Mrs. Kaplan, that when you asked the new question, you got a new answer."

"I did. And something Ida said sent me in the right direction."

"That I said?"

She smiled at me, then addressed Corcoran and Jenkins. "Yes, as has happened so often in the past. Ida said something about how changes in the family can mean changes in the effect of a will, which is why people should update their will from time to time. I asked myself, what would be the effect on Vera's will, and on all that fortune she had, if Daniel were convicted of murdering her. Surely he would not be allowed to keep the money he was given in the will."

Corcoran shook his head. "No, he wouldn't. I'm no lawyer, but I've seen enough of these cases to know that when a beneficiary of a will kills the testator, he isn't allowed to benefit from it."

"Yes, that's what I too learned when I spoke with

the lawyer Farraday, for whom Ida's niece Sara used to work. He told me there is something called a 'slayer statute' that goes into effect in such circumstances."

"And did he tell you what the effect would be on Mrs. Gold's will?" Corcoran asked.

"In general terms he did, as he had not of course seen the will. But I described the family situation as well as I could, and he told me who would be likely to benefit the most from Daniel's conviction."

Both Corcoran and Jenkins were leaning forward now, waiting for the answer.

"And who is that, Mrs. Kaplan?" Jenkins asked.

"Why, Fannie, of course. Her sister and next closest relative, Frances Kleinberg."

Chapter Twenty-Six

We all were silent for at least a minute as we digested this information. Then Inspector Corcoran said, "Now, wait a minute. I realize that you've suggested a way someone could have given Mrs. Gold the sibutramine earlier in the day. But wasn't it Frances— Fannie—the one who first raised the alarm about her sister's death and was responsible for the investigation?"

"Of course," Mrs. K said. "It was not enough to kill her sister. She had to remove Daniel as well, and the easiest way was to make it look as if he had killed his mother. Let the state do the dirty work, yes?"

"Hmmm" was all Corcoran said to that.

"I'm sure she made up that whole *megillah* about her sister suspecting someone was trying to poison her," Mrs. K continued. "Someone she didn't want to name, Fannie said. That was supposed to further point to Vera's son, Daniel, of course."

"So her motive was to get Daniel's inheritance," Corcoran said.

"Yes, but actually there's a little more to it than that. I asked some more questions of both Daniel and Mr. Fred Herrington—you know, Vera's former almost-husband. It seems that Fannie always resented the fact that her older sister, who was adopted, got most of the inheritance from their parents, and now it would be passed on to her son and bypass Fannie again. And of

214

course Vera also received a small fortune from her late husband, Gershon, which also did not sit well with Fannie's jealousy."

"Why didn't Daniel tell us this before?" I asked.

"He said he didn't want to say anything against his aunt, who seemed to have changed her attitude and was now being so good to his mother. Which of course was just an act on her part."

Then something occurred to me that I had totally forgotten. "Wait," I said. "What about it being *Yom Kippur*, and that Vera would not break the fast to take her medicine all day...oh, yes, of course. Never mind."

"Yes," Mrs. K said, "it was Fannie who told us Vera wouldn't eat or take her medicine. And of course that was not true either. And we should have been suspicious right then, because being so religious was not in character for Vera.

"And that reminds me of another thing that Fannie said that, now in hindsight, doesn't—what is the word—doesn't jibe with the way Vera was poisoned. Remember, Ida, how Fannie said Vera had claimed that her medications had perhaps been tampered with?"

"Yes, I remember. She said that was what made Vera think someone was trying to poison her."

"Exactly. But we now know that although Vera was, in a sense, poisoned, it was done with a perfectly untampered-with pill, and it was done only once, because it took only once to cause her heart failure, or whatever it is called."

"Cardiac arrest, I think," said Corcoran.

"Yes, thank you. So in retrospect, even if Vera had been afraid of being poisoned, she would not have noticed any tampered-with medicines, because none was tampered with."

More silence. Again broken by Corcoran. "Okay, I admit you're making a case for Mrs. Gold's sister being the guilty party. But where is the evidence?"

"Well, to begin with, I remember you telling us that one of the nurses noticed a pill on the table next to Vera's bed. And it was not there when she was found deceased. I'm guessing that Fannie gave her that pill in the morning and told her the doctor wanted her to take it late in the afternoon. At least that fits the facts we have."

"Yes," Corcoran said, "but it's still fairly weak evidence."

"I realize that, and I have, in fact, two more pieces of evidence, and each one is better than all of the trout-in-the-milk kind of evidence you have against Daniel."

That certainly seemed to perk both men up, and they leaned even farther forward than already they were. I thought Jenkins might fall onto his *pisk*, his face, which would have been quite funny if the moment were not so serious.

Mrs. K, without a doubt enjoying having such an attentive audience, cleared her throat and continued:

"Believe me, it took me a long time and a lot of thinking before I even considered the possibility that Fannie was guilty, for all the reasons we have already discussed. The timing. The *Yom Kippur* fast. The lack of a motive. And just the fact that I really liked Fannie and had never had any reason to consider her to be anything but a *mensch*. A very fine person who loved her sister. But as Mr. Sherlock Holmes would put it, since I considered Daniel being guilty to be impossible—I know I was probably the only one who thought this, except of course Daniel—I had to consider the possible-but-not-very-likely, including Fannie.

"Learning about the effect of Vera's will if Daniel had been convicted provided the motive. The epiphany about the time-release capsule told me the timing problem probably could be solved. But how would Fannie, who was not a pharmacist like Daniel, get her hands on this…" (here her eyes rolled upwards as she stopped to remember the name and how to pronounce it) "this si-bu-tra-mine?"

"Yes," Corcoran said, "without that piece, it's still just as much circumstantial evidence as that against the son."

"I know that. So I gathered together all of the facts we had so far discovered. All of them, whether they directly related to Fannie or not. And one of those facts concerned Vera's cousin, Erik Weiss."

"You mean the fellow who had been in jail?" Jenkins asked. I was impressed, and a little surprised, that he remembered that name from our previous meeting.

"Yes, that's him. Remember how I had asked you to find the photograph that Vera had shown to Rena Shapiro, a photograph of the whole family from a long time ago?"

"Yes, of course," said Corcoran. "I assumed you wanted to see if you recognized this Erik Weiss, perhaps had seen him lurking in the area."

"Actually, that was not the reason," Mrs. K said. "At least not the main reason. What I wanted was to see an old picture of Fannie Kleinberg. I wanted to know what she looked like ten or fifteen years ago."

"And why was that?" Corcoran asked, looking quite puzzled. I already knew the answer, as Mrs. K had told me, and I was enjoying that the policemen did not, as they say, have a clue.

"Because I suspected that at one time Fannie was quite overweight herself. It is probably a family trait. And I was right. She was quite…quite *zaftig* in those days."

"But Mrs. Gold was extremely slim…"

"Yes, but remember, Vera was adopted. She shared no genetic traits with Fannie."

That certainly silenced the inspector, who nodded. All he said was, "Please continue."

"Thank you. Now Fannie has obviously lost a lot of weight since then. But you may have noticed how her clothes hang loosely on her. I always just assumed, and probably others did as well, that she simply dressed poorly. Bought clothes that didn't fit well. I really should have realized right away what that meant, but to tell the truth, I didn't really think about it much at all. It's not uncommon for older people to wear clothing from a time when they were lighter or heavier, especially if they are not spending much time in the outside world any more, as unfortunately is true of many residents where we live. I guess it's often that we become lighter, we lose weight and even height, with age, although it's sometimes the other way around, as Ida once reminded me." She again smiled in my direction.

"Yes, I'm sure ladies' fashion is a fascinating subject," Corcoran said, not unkindly, "but please get on with your story."

"Certainly. I'm sorry. Where was I?"

Jenkins looked down at his notes. "You were saying that Mrs. Kleinberg had once been overweight. That is what *zaftig* means, I take it." It's clear Jenkins is not missing anything this time either. Good for him.

"Yes, or at least what you would call plump. So if Fannie was once overweight and wanted to reduce, which apparently she did, it's possible she once had a prescription for sibutramine." This time she hardly tripped over the name at all—*Nu*, it is practice making perfect.

"Possible, yes," Corcoran said.

"That's what I said. But how to find out whether what was possible had actually happened? This was the next puzzle. Now there were only three ways I could think of: I could ask you to look back in Fannie's prescription records, which Ida and I decided it was unlikely you would do; I could ask someone else with access to those records to do the same thing; or…well, I'd rather not say what the third way was." I was glad Mrs. K didn't mention anything about the lady burglar. That could have led to several other very uncomfortable questions.

"Well, you didn't ask us," Corcoran said, "which is just as well. Although we might have been able to get that information, it would have required the equivalent of a search warrant, and I probably would have needed more from you than just your suspicion of Mrs. Kleinberg."

"Yes, I realize that, so we didn't ask. Instead I asked D…I asked someone else who had access to these pharmacy records."

Corcoran and Jenkins both now looked as if they were going to say something, but both stopped themselves. Corcoran looked over at Jenkins and gave a tiny shake of his head, and Jenkins nodded slightly in understanding. Corcoran then smiled at us and said,

219

"Okay, we won't ask who. But how did you know what pharmacy would have Mrs. Kleinberg's records?"

"I didn't know. But as she had lived in this state for many years before coming to the Home, and just about everywhere in the state is one of those big Buy & Save Drug Mart stores, I thought there was a good chance that is where Fannie got her prescriptions."

"Hmm. Isn't that where Daniel Gold works?"

"I suppose it is. But we are not going to talk about that, yes?"

"Yes. I mean no. Please continue."

"Well, it turned out Fannie had indeed bought her prescriptions from a Buy & Save Drug store. So maybe you can guess what else I found out?"

Jenkins spoke up again. "That Mrs. Kleinberg had taken sibutramine?" I am becoming all the time more impressed with sourpuss Jenkins.

"Yes, exactly. It was prescribed to her for weight loss, before it was banned and people were warned not to take it, because of the way it affects heart rhythm. I asked Da…I looked up what was said about it at the time, and they said it was especially not to be taken with any other medicine that also affects heart rhythm, because it could be fatal. And of course zipar…zi-pra-si-done— that is hard for me to say—affects heart rhythm. It was one of the drugs people taking sibutramine were specifically warned not to take with it, and especially not take one near the time of taking the other. Anyone taking it would know of this danger."

"You're sure of this?" Corcoran asked.

"I saw the actual warning label."

"Yes, of course. So we have more circumstantial evidence, although I admit it's pretty strong. I don't suppose you found any…any what we might call direct evidence? Like a confession? Or a smoking gun? Or in this case a bottle of pills?"

Mrs. K laughed slightly. "You remember I told you there was another way we considered to get this evidence of the pills? I might have been able to hand you the pills she used, provided she had kept them around. It would, of course, have been *narishkeit*, stupidity, on her part, but as you said regarding finding those pills at Daniel's house, criminals often do such stupid things, almost like keeping a souvenir of their crime. But we didn't go that way, so I cannot hand you the pills. But you say a confession? I may have something just as good."

Corcoran suddenly put up his hand. "You know, Mrs. Kaplan, this is all both fascinating and instructive. You're making an excellent case. I think before you go on, I'll get myself some coffee. Would you ladies like some? No? Tea perhaps? Certainly. Jenkins, give me a hand here."

They both left the office, and I don't think it was just to get coffee. They had left the door open, and I could see they were having what you would call an animated conversation in the outer office, after which Jenkins went to get the drinks but Corcoran went over to his secretary's desk and made a telephone call. A few minutes later they both were back, Jenkins carrying a tray with mugs of coffee and tea on it. We each took our drinks, took a few sips, and then Corcoran said, "That's better. Now, Mrs. Kaplan, if you will continue?"

"Certainly. I think you were saying it would be nice to have maybe a confession by Fannie. I had the same thought, because I knew we still didn't have much more than the kind of evidence you had—and I guess I pooh-

poohed—against Daniel. But of course I was not *meshugge* enough to think Fannie would simply tell me, yes, she killed her sister. So I borrowed Ida's new telephone."

"You were going to get her to confess on the telephone?" Corcoran said. "I don't get it."

"Wait and you will see. At first I thought I would do what those detectives in the television stories do, you know, they confront the suspect and accuse them and the guilty one says something like, 'Okay, I admit it. You've got me. But you can't prove it.' Or maybe he tries to run away, or even attacks the detective. Something like that which proves his guilt. But I realized that usually it doesn't happen that way in real life. If I were to accuse Fannie, she would just deny it. Why shouldn't she, especially if I really can't prove it. And then she would be aware she has been found out and would destroy whatever evidence there was, or maybe try to escape."

"So what did you do?"

"As I said, I borrowed Ida's new telephone. It's one of those smart telephones that does everything."

"Like one of those knives," I put in. I don't think anyone knew what I was talking about, from how they looked at me.

"And one of the things Ida said it would do was to make a recording. Even with pictures if I wanted. So I thought I shall go and talk to Fannie in private. Accuse her of killing Vera. Maybe she will admit it to me, saying I cannot prove it, maybe not. But whatever she says, I will be recording it on Ida's telephone."

"Very clever," Corcoran said. "You'd be, in effect, wearing a wire."

"Is that what they call it? This telephone doesn't

have any wires. Anyway, as I told you, I didn't really think Fannie would admit her crime to me, alone or not. Again, why should she? But I thought I might just get her to say something just as incriminating."

At this point, Mrs. K took my telephone out of her pocket and put it on Corcoran's desk. She touched this place and that, and right away we were hearing what took place when she visited Fannie. I think perhaps it would be clearer if I just insert here for you what they call the transcript of the conversation. It was made by the police and later used at Fannie's trial, and the police were nice enough to let me borrow it.

Mrs. Kaplan: Hello, Fannie, dear. May I come in for a moment?

Frances Kleinberg: Sure. What's up?

K: Do you remember that I told you about those two medicines that combined to cause your sister's death?

F: Yes, what about them?

K: Well, Fannie, it occurred to me that you probably were, well, a *bissel* overweight at one time.

F: So what if I was? What's the point?

K: Well, I thought you might at that time have had a prescription for that weight-loss drug that someone gave to Vera…you know?

F: I don't know what you're talking about.

K: I mean, if you used to take that medicine…

F: You're crazy, you know that? Look, I have never taken sibutramine in my life. And even if I had, it would have been a helluva long

223

time ago. But I didn't. And you must be getting pretty desperate to save that precious Daniel to have the bloody nerve to come here and accuse me of killing my own sister.

That is enough. You get the idea. Fannie then threw Mrs. K out of her apartment, using some very bad language. It gives me chills to read this again and realize that Fannie might have done more than swear at her and throw her out. She was lucky.

Anyway, when Mrs. K finishes, Jenkins says, "I may be missing something, but all I heard was Mrs. Kleinberg denying she gave the fatal medicine to her sister." To Corcoran, he asked, "Did you hear anything else?"

Corcoran was thoughtful. He rubbed his chin. It was like he was trying to figure out a good riddle. Which in a way he was. Then he said to Mrs. K, "Has it got something to do with…with what she knew?"

Mrs. K almost beamed with pleasure. "You are very sharp, Inspector. That is indeed the point. I'm quite certain neither Ida nor I ever mentioned to Fannie the name of the drug that killed her sister. You had told us not to give out many details, and that was one thing I did not mention to anyone, and I doubt other residents knew it either, unless one of you told them. Or Daniel did. And I'm sure he didn't."

"No, no, we didn't let that out, I'm sure." Corcoran scratched his head and shook it a bit. Finally he said, "Is there anything else you want to add? For example, how do you explain the pills found in Daniel's house?"

"Oh, that's easy. For a week after Vera's death, Daniel was sitting *shiva* at his home. He was in mourning. And much of that time, Fannie was there too, as was quite proper. So she had more than enough opportunity to plant that bottle of pills in the back of Daniel's medicine cabinet, where she hoped it would be found by the police."

"You think she expected us to search Daniel's house?"

"Not necessarily, but there was no harm in putting the pills there just in case. In fact, I'll bet she had some plan to tip the police off in some way in case they didn't get the idea on their own."

"Yes, I see," Corcoran said. "Anything else?"

Mrs. K shook her head. "No, that's all. It is my opinion that if the evidence against Daniel is like a trout in the milk, that against Fannie is more like a shark in the soup."

Corcoran laughed. "And is that kosher, Mrs. Kaplan? I thought mixing meat and milk was not permitted for Jews."

"Yes, it is perfectly kosher. Fish is not the same as meat. Just look at the piles of lox and cream cheese at any bar mitzvah."

"Yes, I've actually seen that. All right, you've made your point, as usual. As you can understand, we will have to check out these things you've told us. In fact, I've already got the wheels turning, including bringing Mrs. Kleinberg in for questioning." Aha! That's what he was doing on the telephone while Jenkins was getting the drinks. He had obviously heard enough by then. "As soon as we're done here, I'll be getting a search warrant for her apartment. If what you tell me checks out, well, I think we can drop our case against Daniel Gold. And he'll have you to thank for it.

"And Mrs. Kaplan, I have to say I'm now glad you completely ignored my request that you and Mrs. Berkowitz drop your…your investigation. By now I really should have known better." This sounded very much like what the police usually said to Mr. Sherlock Holmes after they had told him to "butt out," as Mrs. K had put it, and he had then solved the case for them.

"Thank you very much, Inspector," Mrs. K said graciously. "Ida and I are very pleased we were able to help. I will wait to hear what you find out."

We all stood up. Jenkins was scratching his head. Suddenly he put out his hand to shake Mrs. K's and said, "I've gotta admit that was pretty damn impressive, Mrs. Kaplan."

Such a statement coming from the *shlumper* Jenkins was even more impressive, if you ask me.

****

As we left the police building, feeling many pounds lighter than when we entered, I said to Mrs. K, "Tell me, Rose: When you said you might consider asking the burglar lady to help us again, what did you have in mind? Surely not that she would sneak into the Buy & Save Drug Mart store and steal the records?"

Mrs. K laughed. "No, nothing like that. If I couldn't get the prescription records somehow, I wanted her to enter Fannie's room and look for the bottle of diet pills from which she gave one to Vera."

"You thought she would still have that bottle?"

"Well, as we just were saying, it's not uncommon for the criminal to make a mistake like that, to overlook or leave behind some evidence of his crime, perhaps because he was so sure he wouldn't be suspected or caught. I thought it was a chance worth taking. But I'm

226

glad we didn't have to take it."

"As am I," I said. I thought it very unlikely Fannie would have made such a mistake. To be honest, however, I can tell you now that when the police eventually searched Fannie's apartment, they did indeed find a bottle with the remaining pills. She had put some in Daniel's house, but she had kept the prescription bottle from which they came, even with its label. It was very careless of Fannie, especially after it seemed Mrs. K suspected her, but no doubt she either forgot she still had the pills, or she dismissed Mrs. K as a busybody no one would believe, especially because she still seemed to lack both a motive and an opportunity. But as Mrs. K would say, her being guilty was not the impossible of Mr. Sherlock Holmes's famous advice.

It was just the improbable that turned out to be the truth.

We walked a little farther before I thought of something else. "One other thing I forgot to ask, Rose. Where did this cousin Erik fit in? I mean, was he at the Home or not? Did he also try to kill Vera?"

Mrs. K stopped and turned to me. "I'm so sorry, Ida. I completely forgot to tell you. Inspector Corcoran telephoned me yesterday and said the police had picked up Erik Weiss somewhere in town here and questioned him. He admitted coming to the Home on *Yom Kippur*. It turns out he was not a murderer, just a *shnorrer*—a moocher—every family has one. He wanted to ask Vera for money. He hoped he could make her feel guilty enough, especially on the Day of Atonement, for testifying against him that she would give him something, maybe just to make him go away. Anyway, when he found out she was so sick, he figured he would not be able to carry out his plan and left."

"And the police believed him?"

"Yes, I think so. It was never very likely that he gave Vera the medicine anyway, was it? How would he do it? Where would he get sibutramine, unless perhaps he too once had taken it?" She was getting very good at saying the name now. "But mostly, what would he gain, except revenge? He was not in the will, whatever happened to Daniel. And he was not known as a violent criminal, just an embezzler. So yes, I think they believed him.

"And now that Daniel will be inheriting almost all of Vera's money, no doubt he will be the next relative the *shnorrer* Erik visits. And if I know Daniel, he will give him something. A kind heart he has."

And so it was back to the Julius and Rebecca Cohen Home for Jewish Seniors. Like most such places, it can be a rather dull and unexciting place much of the time.

But life there is never boring for too long when your best friend is Rose Kaplan.

A word about the author…

Mark Reutlinger is the author of the novels MADE IN CHINA, MURDER WITH STRINGS ATTACHED, and SISTER-IN-LAW (under the pen name M. R. Morgan), as well as two other Mrs. Kaplan Mysteries, MRS. KAPLAN AND THE MATZOH BALL OF DEATH and OY VEY, MARIA!. A Professor of Law Emeritus at Seattle University, Reutlinger was born in San Francisco, graduated from UC Berkeley (where he was awarded the University Gold Medal), and now lives with his wife, Analee, in University Place, Washington.

Thank you for purchasing
this publication of The Wild Rose Press, Inc.

For questions or more information
contact us at
info@thewildrosepress.com.

The Wild Rose Press, Inc.
www.thewildrosepress.com